FIRST SPARK

PHOENA'S QUEST BOOK 1

Chrissy Garwood/Chrisolite Books

Sorell, Tasmania, Australia, 7172

www.chrissygarwood.com

Cover Design: Donita Bundy

First Spark: Phoena's Quest Book 1/ Chrissy Garwood. —1st ed.

ISBN 978-0- 6485434-8-0 (paperback)
    978-0-6485434-9-7 (eBook)

FIRST SPARK

PHOENA'S QUEST
BOOK I

CHRISSY GARWOOD

CHRISOLITE BOOKS

Sorell, Tasmania, Australia

Dedicated to my Great-Niece, Ella.

CONTENTS

PRONUNCIATION GUIDE

Phoena – *fee-nah*
Oramis – o-ram-is (short o as in hop)
Baraapa – bar-ah-pah
Karilion – kar-ill-yon
Heilga – hey-el-gah

CHAPTER I:
INTRODUCTIONS

Phoena approached the apartment door at the end of the windowless hallway, still puzzled by her instructions. She rechecked her pocket for the ornate metal key. Why did Matron tell her to choose her words carefully?

A senior maid had taken ill, and the timid teenager was the only housemaid available to complete the work. Matron had complained about sixteen-year-old Phoena's unsuitability, but all the experienced servants were committed to essential preparations for the new semester. After reminding Phoena not to dawdle, Matron had reluctantly presented her with a temporary key.

This was Phoena's first visit to the fourth floor, and she was alone in the wing reserved for the wealthier students. She read the brass panels on the doors as she passed – proud names and noble titles. Students attending the *Westernbrooke Academy for Young Noblemen* came from throughout the Western Empire. The boarding school even drew students from beyond the Five Seas...

A row of bright candelabra, suspended near the ceiling, lit her way like a procession of accusers. The morning was half gone, and the whirr of her equipment trolley as it traversed the polished boards disrupted the silence. Her assignment must be finished before eleven.

Phoena stopped her trolley, confirming that the apartment number matched the engraving on the key. At first glance, the door looked like any other, although it lacked a nameplate to identify the owner. But this school had magic, alchemy and sorcery on the curriculum–

She scolded herself; it was the younger students who set magical traps. This floor was reserved for the senior students.

With a satisfying click, the key slipped into the lock, but then it refused to turn. She grabbed the handle and pushed, but the door did not yield. Nothing she tried would persuade the key to budge or the door to open.

Battling tears, Phoena crouched beside the lock. "What do you have against me, door?" she whispered. "I didn't ask to be sent here—"

The key jiggled in the lock, and she leapt back. Magical mischief!

Phoena chewed her lip and took a deep breath. "Open up, door. Matron sent me!"

Her voice echoed along the empty hallway. The key moved, and the mechanism released itself with a loud bang. Before she could retrieve the key, it disappeared in a puff of blue smoke. Shaken, the servant girl pushed the door open. The hinges creaked as if they snickered at her entry.

Phoena pushed her cleaning trolley across the threshold. Seconds flew by while she waited for something else to happen. The room was overheated and stuffy, the only light coming from a huge blaze in the massive fireplace across the room. Seizing her courage, the girl rushed forward to deal with the fire. She attacked the logs with the poker, pushing them apart to diminish the inferno. Why had the fourth-year student who lodged here thrown so much fuel on the fire?

The unknown nobleman's actions would force Phoena to delay cleaning the fireplace. Matron had outlined a strict schedule, with no margin for compromise. Failing to clean the hearth might lead to a demotion – or something worse. She shuddered. Being a housemaid was much preferred to slaving in the kitchens. Where would she go if Matron dismissed her from the household staff at this exclusive boarding school? The *Westernbrooke Academy* was the only home the orphan had ever known.

The skinny girl tugged on heavy curtains that hung either side of the hearth. She uncovered huge windows to let in the morning light. Her jaw dropped at the sight of landscaped gardens extending towards a sparkling river. She lifted the sash windows, and wasted precious seconds welcoming a refreshing breeze.

Shaking herself, Phoena went towards her trolley. She had left the hallway door open beyond it, but while her back was turned, it had closed. She ran to the door and tugged on the handle – locked again. Tempted to vent her frustration on the door, she opened her mouth, but then the clock on the mantle began to chime. Ten o'clock!

Forcing herself to refocus on her deadline, the maid moved to the next task. With a bundle of beeswax tapers in her hand, she rushed back to the mantelpiece and came to a sudden halt. Pristine candles with white wicks filled all the silver candlesticks. She spun to survey the room. None of the candles needed replacing. Had someone already been here? Her eyes searched the room, noting the discarded goblets and scattered cushions. No self-respecting maid would replace candles and leave the sitting room in such disarray. That must mean the young nobleman had another method for illuminating his apartment. She took a deep breath – more magic!

Phoena tidied the sitting room before moving to a door on the left. Through a dark hallway, she accessed two bedrooms. Each had a separate dressing room, with a marble-lined bathroom shared between them. After opening the curtains in every room, it was easier to ignore the unused candles.

Only one of the bedrooms was in use, but His Lordship must have abandoned his rooms in haste. She wrestled fresh bed linen into place on the enormous canopied bed, before retrieving discarded pillows. In the bathroom, tepid water filled the tub. Ivory combs and shaving equipment were spread beside the hand basin, and abandoned towels dumped on the floor.

A mountain of discarded clothes in the dressing room threatened to become an avalanche. Phoena dispatched the soiled items into the laundry bag on her trolley – it bore the individual room number. Then armfuls of clean clothes went into the wardrobes.

She hunted across the room for the partners to four mismatched boots, vigorously applying polish until she could see her reflection in the leather. When she placed them in a tall cupboard, she found more boots that required similar attention.

All these possessions belonged to a single nobleman.

The clock on the sitting room mantelpiece chimed the half-hour, and Phoena shook her head. Ten-thirty already.

Returning to the sitting room, she hurried to the door in the opposite wall. It opened into a book-lined study furnished with a roll-top wooden desk and half a dozen padded armchairs. Scrunched balls of paper were scattered around the small wastebasket, and several leather-bound books lay tossed onto the floor.

A vast array of equipment lay on open shelves waiting for her to dust it. Most of these items she had only seen behind glass, in locked cabinets, downstairs in the alchemy classrooms.

When nothing remained on her list but the fire, Phoena knelt beside the ornate brick hearth. She stared at the red-hot coals, frowning at the thick layers of ash underneath them. There was too much powdery residue. It would have to be halved to prevent the fire from being smothered. The roaring blaze had burned down to half its intensity, but it was still too hot. Watching the dancing flames, she wiped the perspiration from her brow. A tear trickled down her cheek, and she brushed it away. What folly to think she could prove her worth to Matron!

Shouts of excitement drifted up from the garden. The students were taking advantage of their free time. Formal lessons were not scheduled to start for another week. Phoena glanced towards the open windows. Mid-morning sunshine streamed into the room.

Pushing up her sleeves, Phoena gritted her teeth and began shovelling aside the fiery coals as she dug for the cooler ashes in the grate. With her bucket almost full, she began to relax, but then a smouldering log shifted and the careful balance was lost. Ignoring the exploding sparks, the maid attacked the rolling logs with her tools. She saved the hearthrug. Not a single glowing coal escaped the confines of the hearth, but she grimaced over a painful blister rising on her palm.

Her childhood had been spent tending the huge kitchen fires at the *Academy*. In that harsh environment, where survival had depended on taming the flames, a small burn had been a minor concern. The cook had thrashed her if anything burnt in the ovens, or if the roasting temperatures were wrong.

"Be thankful life in the kitchen is behind you," she whispered. "And be grateful those skills helped you deal with this blaze." The full bucket sat on the hearth while she double-checked the apartment. Phoena closed the sitting room windows and sighed. The clock had not chimed eleven, but if she couldn't get past the door...

The bucket was too hot for the trolley. Phoena wrapped a thick cloth around the handle before she raised it from the spotless hearth. With the bucket in her right hand, the maid grasped the trolley with her left, frowning towards the locked door. She was only a step from the hearth when she froze.

The handle on that impossible door moved, and without a sound it began to swing open.

Trembling, the teenager returned the bucket to the hearth. She bobbed down and peered around her trolley, her mind fixated on the spell books and mystical paraphernalia in the study.

Hide me, she silently prayed, holding her breath. She scrunched her eyes shut and waited.

The door closed.

"Hide me," a voice whispered, "under the shadow of your wings."

Phoena's heart pounded in her chest. She had never heard anyone else at this *Academy* speak the words of that prayer. When she had made the mistake of saying it aloud many years ago, the cook had almost killed her with his fists.

As a child, she hadn't understood his hate-filled words. Why had he tagged her as part of the "elitist minority" who devoted themselves to an "obsolete religion"? Could this new arrival answer those forgotten questions? She strained to hear more.

The room felt empty, except for a quiet sound, like a moth fluttering near a flame. The teenager opened her eyes as a shadowy blur launched itself into the ash-filled bucket on the hearth. She gasped. Some kind of creature was burrowing beneath the smouldering coals. There was a flash of red flame, and then no further movement. For an insane moment, she contemplated upending the bucket. A tear escaped the corner of her eye. Phoena chided herself for being a sentimental fool. Rising to her feet, she seized the handle of the bucket with both hands, preparing to flee.

With a bang, the hallway door burst inward. Three young noblemen pushed into the room. They stopped short when they saw Phoena standing there, with the smouldering bucket in her hands. Their darker complexions and their clothes suggested they were wealthy international students.

All three had beards, a privilege reserved for senior students. Two wore their dark curly hair close-cropped to their heads, while the shortest one had a thick mane.

"Where is he?" the shorter student demanded.

He spoke with authority, but she knew he couldn't be the owner of this room. The family portraits on the wall didn't match. Had the first intruder left the door unlocked? Or was there more magic at work here?

The spokesman strode towards her, his eyes darting around the room as he dragged her to the centre. "Where's the nobleman who came through this door?"

Phoena dropped into an awkward curtsey.

She kept her eyes downcast. "I saw no nobleman." In her mind, she rehearsed the mantra that always guided her: *A good servant is quiet, invisible, obedient, trustworthy and faithful. A good servant is...*

The other young men searched the sitting room. At first, they looked in the obvious hiding places. When their efforts went unrewarded, they became more frantic. Phoena quaked at the sound of their chaos when they went into the other rooms. She desperately kept hold of the bucket.

"Baraapa, he's not here," one of the others said.

The youth who held her nodded, looking directly into her eyes. They were the same height, but she felt insignificant in his presence.

"Where did he go?" Baraapa's breath was warm on her face, and his grip tightened on her arm. "We saw him come in. Did you see how he magicked himself out of this room?"

She frowned, gnawing her bottom lip. Would this nobleman believe her if she told him the truth?

The tension increased. He raised his hand as if to strike her. It had been five years since anyone had hit her. The girl's eyes closed and her mind recoiled, but her body remained motionless.

The blow never came. Seconds turned to minutes. His grip on her arm didn't lessen, but the small nobleman had stopped moving. Phoena opened her eyes.

His companions cried out with concern because he resembled a statue. Drops of perspiration appeared on his brow as Baraapa stared at his upraised hand. In his wide eyes, she saw fear and confusion, not the anger she expected.

A spark of hope ignited within her.

But then the hallway door opened a third time.

Everyone turned towards the tall youth who entered. Her attacker came to himself with a shudder and dropped his hand.

The newcomer asked, "What are you doing in *my* room?"

His arrival changed the atmosphere. Everything about him declared his great wealth and privilege. His thick, shoulder-length hair and trimmed beard were dark like theirs, but his skin was fair. He was one of this kingdom's aristocracy. His tailored clothes accentuated his muscular physique. More imposing in stature than the three foreign students, he towered over them.

The youth who held Phoena dropped his hands as he bowed to the owner of the room. Momentarily forgotten, the girl slipped back towards the hearth, where she set down the heavy bucket. With her chin down, she longed to become invisible. The three interlopers shuffled their feet.

"We were chasing Oramis – the Emberite," Baraapa said. "We saw him come in here, but there's no trace of him now."

"Was it necessary to trash my room?"

"Sorry, Karilion. We were going to ask the maid to tidy it for you."

"Is that what you were doing?" Karilion asked. "Don't you know that maids are more forthcoming if you don't threaten them with the back of your hand. You! Girl! What is your name?"

Phoena risked a glance at Lord Karilion.

He was even more handsome than he appeared in the portrait on the wall. He crossed the room, frowning as she peered up at him. He reached out his hand. A lock of her brown hair had fallen loose from her bun. He twisted this hair around his fingers while his dark eyes studied her and his lips curled into a charming smile.

Her face flushed as she made the connection between his actions and his name. This young man had a scandalous reputation. She could feel the heat from the fire behind her and dared not retreat any further, without risking her long skirt to the flames.

"Your name," Karilion repeated. His self-assured grin declared there was no option but for her to comply. His other hand reached for her waist.

Phoena slipped sideways and bobbed an apology. The young lord seemed surprised.

"I'm s-sorry, Your Lordship... but... Matron will be... l-looking for me." She grabbed the ash bucket with both arms and held it close like a shield, ignoring the heat. "I-I don't want... any trouble. I didn't... s-see... any nobleman come in... and I-I... have to go!"

The other young men were standing between Phoena and the door. She threw a desperate glance towards them. Karilion laughed. "You three, let her pass. Open the door." They hastened to obey.

After stepping into the hallway, she walked swiftly away. Was it fear or self-preservation that kept her from running? The wide hall was busy with students returning from their morning activities. They came in groups of three and four, jostling and jousting with each other. This made it difficult for Phoena to pass without attracting more unwelcome stares.

With each step, her expectation grew that someone would pursue her. By the time she reached the safety of the servants' stairs, her outer calm was a flimsy facade. As soon as she was sure she was out of sight, her feet raced onward. Only when she was on the ground floor did Phoena lean against the wall to catch her breath.

Her heart pounded, and the pain along both arms was almost unbearable. Abandoning her trolley had been a terrible mistake. Setting the hot metal bucket down on the freshly scrubbed flagstones was a punishable offence.

Overwhelmed by her narrow escape, she closed her eyes.

"Trouble seems to follow *you* wherever you go." Matron's words brought the maid back to full alert in an instant.

The maid's eyes flew open, and the colour fled from her face.

There was no need for Matron to say anything further. The older woman's frown – and the smug nobleman standing at her side – was sufficient.

Lord Karilion grinned, before raising his hand in the air. "You left in such haste you forgot your trolley."

Phoena blinked, as her cleaning trolley magically appeared in the space between them.

"I-I'm sorry, sir," the maid said, curtseying under Matron's stony glare.

"I can assure you, My Lord," Matron said, "*this* girl will cause you no further trouble."

"You misunderstand my intentions," Karilion said. Matron's expression suggested she did not agree with his claim. He laughed. "I've not come to complain. There have been some intruders in my room, and I need this maid to return to tidy my apartment."

Matron frowned at him. The intimidating woman drew herself to her full height. She was formidable in her black gown and white cap, and her foot tapped impatiently. "That is impossible, My Lord." She crossed her arms over her ample chest. "This girl has commitments elsewhere."

"Ah." Karilion flashed another charming smile. "Then I will take my leave, Matron."

He walked away without a backward glance.

"I didn't expect him to give up so easily," Matron muttered. She nodded towards Phoena's trolley. This unspoken instruction was familiar. The girl took command of her equipment while her superior left in the opposite direction.

Taking a deep breath, the unsettled teenager half-turned. The space beside her had been empty, but now her way was barred. Karilion smiled. She looked frantically around. The few passing servants seemed not to notice her dilemma.

"Your name," he whispered in her ear. "Then I will petition Headmaster Pepperbry and have Matron's decision overturned."

Her answer escaped. "No!"

"You should be nice to me," he said, cupping her chin in his hand. "When the other students learn what occurred in my room this morning..."

The sixteen-year-old shivered, having endured more than her share of practical jokes. But none of the younger students had ever brought their mischief into the servants' corridor. She stepped further away. "Nothing happened."

"My point exactly," he laughed. "First, you dispatched the new student, that Emberite, with your magic. And then you held off three established fourth-years who were tracking him. I wonder what you would have done to *them* if I hadn't arrived when I did."

Phoena frowned.

Everyone knew magic was a passport to freedom and fortune. Any servants with magical talent were recruited to serve the King's Council in the Citadel.

"I don't have any magic."

"Oh ho, so you deny it." He mocked her with his eyes. "And now you've cast a spell over me. Why else am I behaving like a besotted knave in your presence?"

He reached for her, but Phoena ducked out of his reach, still clutching her ash bucket.

"So that's how you want to play this game." He laughed. "I must warn you, the chase is half the fun."

With a click of his fingers, he disappeared.

"You're playing with fire," one of the footmen muttered as he went past. "I don't know what you've done to attract His Lordship's attention. But don't stand there with your mouth open. Matron won't be happy to learn that he returned."

After moving the bucket to her hip, Phoena visited the laundry before pushing her trolley to the storeroom. No one said anything, but she caught several maids snickering. She continued to glance over her shoulder.

Lord Karilion did not reappear.

Finally, she escaped to the back garden with the bucket. She checked for anyone working among the garden beds. A high timber barrier concealed the ash heap from the main building. After wending her way towards the rear, Phoena was confident she had the furthest corner to herself and ducked around this screen. With great care, she upended the bucket. What would be left of the mysterious creature she had wanted to rescue?

A cloud of grey ash arose as she dispersed the dying embers. Covering her nose and mouth with her apron, she grabbed a sturdy stick. When disappointment extinguished her fleeting hope, she dropped the stick. Phoena straightened and reached for the bucket.

A small noise drew her back to the ashes. Where did that puff of smoke come from? Phoena stared. The abandoned stick burst into flame. Something shiny and black moved beneath the newly lit fire. At first, it was tiny, no larger than a beetle. It grew and grew while she waited.

The creature was longer than her forearm, its body round like the cook's overfed cat. Then it unwound itself. It had both a long, tapered tail and a serpentine neck.

She tiptoed closer. All movement ceased. The growing stopped. A bearded head swivelled towards her on the long neck, two shiny red eyes glaring at her. What kind of monster was this? The thing shrieked, unfurling delicate wings. She gasped. It flew towards her, hissing and spitting. The creature was agile, but Phoena was desperate to find out what it was. She wrestled with it until she stumbled. Her legs collapsed, throwing her onto her back. She hit the ground hard.

The creature wriggled from her grasp and she scrambled to recapture it. When the thing stopped struggling, Phoena sat down and brought the beast closer to her face. Unblinking crimson eyes held her prisoner, and she forgot how to breathe.

It resembled a lizard, except it had long fur like a collar above the shoulders, and a mane around its head. The tapered tail was twice as long as its body. A pair of translucent wings sprouted from the shoulders. The triangular-shaped head ended in a blunt snout. The animal opened its mouth to reveal a double row of pointy teeth.

"You're beautiful," she whispered.

A shiver ran through the creature. Had it understood her words? It blew a puff of smoke from its snout. The smoke was followed by a flicker of flame. "You're a tiny dragon," she cried. It chirped as if it was answering her.

Taken by surprise, Phoena lost her grip. The creature dropped into her lap. Too small to be a dragon, she would call him a "dragonet".

The dragonet hissed at her with orange flames when she extended her right hand towards it. A small cry escaped her lips as her already-blistered palm reacted to the heat. Phoena bit her fist. A scream at this hour would bring someone from the kitchen to investigate.

With tear-filled eyes, she examined the angry blister. The dragonet clawed its way along her arm, holding its head as if it also studied the injury. Then the small head darted forward. Before she could blink, it sank its tiny teeth into the painful blister.

Phoena choked on her scream, shaking her arm, but the dragonet would not let go. She swatted at him with her other hand. The long tail twisted in the air, binding both her limbs together. The dragonet's scales changed colour, rippling in waves of black and red. Both her arms pulsed in agony to match the rhythm.

Phoena was crying, quivering from the pain. "You little beast. Now I'll have to go to the Infirmary. It will cost me all my savings. I wish I'd never found you."

The tail unwound from her arms. She leapt backwards, flinging the creature from her. It floated in the air, the wings holding it steady, and then it flew to her shoulder.

The pain was suddenly gone! Phoena shook her head in disbelief.

She held up her healed palm and compared it with her other one. She examined her arms. Where was the scorched redness from holding the hot bucket too long? There was no sign that she had burnt herself.

"How did you do that?" she asked.

The dragonet blew a puff of flame at her, rising into the air and hovering before her face.

"I don't understand—" Phoena dropped into her best curtsey. "B-but... th-thank you."

The dragonet chirped before flying over the top of the screen. The maid raced around the wooden barrier to see where the creature would go. It disappeared in the direction of the nearby village and freedom, and she smiled.

When she could no longer see the creature, Phoena returned for her empty bucket. She checked the sun. It was almost overhead. There was no time to delay. She must not be late for her next assignment – the dining hall. She groaned when she remembered the state of her apron.

Those black sooty marks would be impossible to brush off, and the pocket had ripped. She wrapped the apron around the bucket to hide the damage. If she hurried, there might still be time to retrieve a clean apron and have a proper wash.

CHAPTER 2:
TROUBLE IN THE DINING ROOM

The service area, between the kitchen and the closed doors to the dining room, was bustling with activity. Phoena slipped into the service area, alert for the right opportunity to join the maids jostling for position near the counter. She must avoid being seen by Matron, who stood on the other side of the room beside a line of uniformed footmen. This was the first time the teenager had been late, but she had seen this manoeuvre executed by others. The maids wore identical uniforms, and nobody seemed to notice the slender girl's arrival.

As she pressed towards the counter, Phoena glanced at the waiting trolleys. One of the senior maids was glaring in her direction. Heilga pursed her lips and raised two fingers. That signal meant Phoena must collect two meals to make up for lost time. The maid at the front of the line collected a single cloche-covered plate before moving away.

Phoena's heart quaked as she steeled herself for the challenge to come. She was confident that she could carry multiple small vessels without catastrophe, but the luncheon plates were much heavier. She pushed aside her fears as she watched the junior chefs working on the kitchen side of the narrow counter. She recognised each one, but doubted any of them remembered her.

Now there was only one maid ahead of her.

It was mechanical ingenuity, not magic, that propelled the luncheon plates along the counter from one chef's station to the next. Phoena had experienced firsthand the exhausting effort required to crank the handle that worked the conveyer belt. She reined in her memories.

Today, the first young chef dropped thick slices of roast lamb onto the passing plates. Another served crisp, golden potatoes beside the meat. He exercised great care, as did the two apprentices who added steaming vegetables.

To complete the meal, a cascade of rich gravy issued from a white jug. The master of the kitchen – the dreaded man who refused any title other than "Cook" – glowered over everyone's shoulders. At the end of the line, a final chef waited to cover the meal with a domed cloche.

A spot of gravy splashed onto the counter. Phoena's eyes widened, and she held her breath. Time slowed. The stain disappeared with a furtive swipe of an apron. The obese kitchen overlord raised his arm and roared. The offending youth cried out as a heavy ladle struck him across the shoulder before Cook hurled him from the counter.

A collective silence fell, but service continued. The plate received a cover and was carried away. Phoena advanced to the head of the queue. The plate she needed crept towards the gravy jug, which had dropped to the counter with a thud. Another junior chef materialised in time to add gravy to the plate, and now the last man held it towards her.

"I need another one, please," Phoena said in a clear voice, as she balanced the plate in the crook of her arm. When the chef hesitated, the girl added, "I have my orders."

Cook grunted his approval and the second plate was offered to her. As Phoena retreated to the relative safety of Heilga's trolley, she avoided looking towards Matron. Heilga snatched one plate from her hand, muttering, "Ungrateful wretch, you're late."

"I'm sorry," Phoena said, passing her the second plate.

"There's no time for excuses," Heilga said, "Get back into line. We have a full table."

That information increased the urgency. How unlucky to have a full table! She had been hoping that there might only be three or four seated at their table today. Not all the students had returned from the semester break, and there had only been sixty students at breakfast. Phoena distracted herself by rehearsing the numbers while she waited for her turn. Maximum capacity for *Westernbrooke Academy* was one hundred and forty-four students.

When it was her turn at the counter again, the second

plate was offered without hesitation. At the end of her sixth trip, Heilga's frown had been replaced with a smile. Phoena closed her eyes while she caught her breath.

"We're not the last team finished," Heilga said. "And I've proved my point. You can carry two plates without mishap. No more excuses. I knew there was hidden talent under that plain exterior, which is why I asked for you to be assigned to work with me."

Matron rang a bell, and the uniformed footmen stepped to the counter. They collected covered dishes and marched with them into the dining hall. The masters were always served first. In a few minutes, the bell would ring again. It would then be time to serve the students.

A loud clatter sounded deep within the cavernous kitchen. Cook's strident voice screamed obscenities at a "wretched" scullery maid. Phoena shuddered in horror. She held her breath and stilled her trembling hands. There was no forgetting the abuse she had suffered while she had been one of those scullery maids. Her rescue from the kitchen, five years ago, had been unexpected.

The teenager still feared that she might be sent back at any moment.

No one could tell Phoena how she had come to live at the *Westernbrooke Academy for Young Noblemen*. In this place, status was important, even among the servants. It determined how everyone would treat you and prescribed how the students behaved towards you. Uncertain parentage was a terrible disadvantage, guaranteeing a bleak future.

The memories were powerful. She had expected to end her days in the kitchen. She was three when she arrived. At first, she had been too small to do anything other than tend the fires, a task she had delighted in. When she could reach the kitchen workbenches, other labour-intensive tasks had been added to her workload.

"Fee," Heilga hissed. "I'm talking to you. Pay attention. As your only friend, you should give me more consideration."

"I'm sorry."

"That's your second apology. What is *wrong* with you today?"

"I had a challenging morning."

Heilga snickered. "That's an understatement."

Phoena looked at her in surprise.

Heilga checked to see who might be listening. "I hear you had a *little* trouble with some of the fourth-years." She spoke loud enough for nearby servants to hear. "Rumour has it you cast a disappearing spell on the Emberite Ambassador's son."

"I didn't!"

Matron rang the bell a second time. All the teams moved towards the dining hall. This prevented any further discussion. Phoena had forgotten to ask about their table assignment. She would have to watch the senior maid carefully.

Heilga had high expectations. They had been paired together for the past three weeks. Her new friend had said there was doubt about whether Phoena was worthy of her place in the dining hall.

Phoena entered the dining hall with her back to the diners. She didn't need to look where she was going. She had memorised the table layout. She kept her eyes on Heilga. The noisy students would be standing. On the right, a long table ran along an elevated platform. This was where the masters sat. Behind each master, a footman awaited the signal to uncover their meals.

The masters always faced the students. The students' tables were arranged in four parallel rows, at right angles to the masters' table. During the semester, there were twelve students at each table – six on either side. They assembled by seniority, with the first-years furthest from the masters. Phoena prayed that Heilga would steer them to the left.

The bell sounded. With a clatter, the students took their seats.

"Table Two," Heilga declared, veering towards the right. Phoena gripped the trolley handle with white knuckles. She felt sick. Table Two was directly in front of the headmaster.

She was more familiar with the tables on the other side

of the room. The first-year boys were rowdy but predictable. Phoena was still learning to cope with the middle section, where Heilga's team had been relegated until her new partner proved herself worthy.

The second- and third-year students were more proficient at magic. This increased the teenager's dread, but they were less interested in playing tricks on the servants. They preferred scoring points off each other instead.

Memories of her only encounter with the fourth-years slowed her steps. It would be most unlucky if she was serving at Lord Karilion's table today.

"Be on your best behaviour," Heilga warned. "These fourth-years richly reward their favourite servants."

Phoena worried about the eagerness in her friend's voice. At twenty-nine, Heilga was one of the older maids. The teenager was still puzzled over this woman's unsought offer of friendship.

The trolley rolled to a stop before Headmaster Pepperbry. This was the closest that Phoena had come to this influential man. She prayed that he would fail to notice her. Heilga was already serving the first two students. Phoena hastened to follow her lead. She placed one plate on the table and turned to serve the second student. At that moment, a familiar voice spoke.

"This is an unexpected honour," Lord Karilion declared to his friends. "Behold the enchantress who serves at our table. Be careful not to meet her eye, lest she mesmerises you."

An expectant hush fell over the diners at his table. Phoena's cheeks reddened. She hesitated for a moment before placing the plate before her tormentor. Refusing to look at him, she continued her duties around the table. When she was directly opposite him, Karilion spoke again, gesturing to the pale, blond man she was about to serve.

"I can't believe you're treating your recent victim as a stranger."

She glanced towards the unfamiliar youth, certain she had never seen him before. He lacked a beard, except for a pale wisp of hair on his chin. Even his thin moustache seemed insubstantial. This made him stand out among his companions. Phoena looked towards Karilion in confusion.

"You must tell us, Oramis," Lord Karilion said, "how she bound you to her will. You have a reputation for being a skilled sorcerer. What did she do to make you vanish?"

A ripple of laughter ran around the table.

"What makes you think I didn't transport myself out of your apartment?"

Phoena froze with the plate hovering just above the table. That was the voice she had heard immediately before the tiny dragon had leapt into her bucket.

"I have defences in place that make that impossible."

Unable to control her curiosity, she glanced at Lord Oramis. The blond nobleman shrugged. "I'm sorry, dear maid, I tried to cover for you. But rest assured, a gentleman never reveals a maiden's secrets."

The blond youth's hand brushed her fingers as Oramis took the plate from her. A surge of heat ran up her arm at his touch. *She mustn't stare!* He was dressed completely in black. His only ornament was a shiny brooch – a coiled dragon pinned to his broad chest. Someone across the table coughed. Phoena blinked and wrenched her eyes from the brooch.

Karilion frowned at her. A wild survey of the table revealed he was not the only one watching this exchange. Phoena could not leave fast enough.

Heilga steered the trolley back to the service area. Phoena busied herself collecting the desserts. These delicacies went on the top. The lower shelves were reserved for the used plates. Too soon, the maids re-entered the dining hall, joining the other servants along the wall to await Matron's next signal.

"Well done, Fee," Heilga chuckled, as soon as they parked their trolley. "It's always a great game when one of the maids captures the attention of these young lords. The fourth-years make everything a do-or-die competition."

Phoena threw her friend a startled look. She opened her

mouth to ask what Heilga meant but her companion pushed her forward. "He's summoning you."

Across the room, Karilion had his goblet raised. He beckoned towards her.

"I'd be careful with that one," a nearby maid said. "More than one girl has ruined her reputation with him."

A chill ran through Phoena. Her eyes flew to Matron, who nodded severely. Phoena selected a carafe of red wine. Her leaden feet approached the table. She filled Karilion's cup and then ran her eyes around the table. Oramis drained his goblet and raised it towards her. She circled the table to fill his cup, hopeful that she concealed her growing unrest.

"I propose a little wager, Oramis," Karilion announced. He brought a leather pouch from his pocket. The coins within jingled with promise. The dark-haired lord tipped a handful of coins into his palm. "See how our enchantress favours neither of us with a smile. I'll wager ten gold medallions that you cannot persuade her to kiss you before she pledges herself to me." He lined the coins along the centre of the table for all to see. Then he drew the cord tight and waved his still-bulging purse before them.

"I'm reluctant to accept your wager." Contrary to his words, Oramis matched each gold coin from a purse. "I'm certain she already finds me more appealing than you. Didn't you see how she couldn't tear her eyes away from me? It doesn't seem fair to rob you of your gold when I've already won."

Then Oramis took out an eleventh coin. He flipped this coin high towards the ceiling. All eyes watched its progress as it descended. The blond youth snatched the coin from the air and held it towards her. She clutched the wine carafe even tighter, stepping back. This coin was more than she would earn in a year.

"If you accept this coin, everyone will know that you prefer me. There's no need for me to embarrass you by demanding a public kiss."

Phoena flinched at his bold assurance. If only she hadn't noticed the glittering dragon-shaped brooch. Her curiosity about a possible connection with the mysterious dragonet had complicated everything. Now she had two students to avoid.

Without a word, she walked stiffly back to Heilga. Laughter chased her all the way. Her heart insisted she should run, but she had won that battle. With downcast eyes, she wished she truly had a disappearing spell. When she reached her friend, Phoena pressed back against the wall.

"You look as if you're going to faint," Heilga said.

Matron appeared in front of her. "Quick, Heilga! Get her out of the dining hall and into the fresh air. You have ten minutes to get her presentable."

"What was that about?" Heilga asked as she hustled Phoena through the side entrance into the back garden.

"A wager."

"A wager," Heilga cried in delight. "What fun! Which lord will you choose?"

"What?"

"Which lord will you favour? Oh, you fortunate girl. They're both wealthy, and they will shower you with expensive gifts. Be careful not to make your choice too soon."

"I'm not selling my kisses," Phoena protested, shaking her head. She wrapped her arms around her trembling body. "I'm not."

Heilga stared at her in astonishment. "You're a strange one, Fee. Presented with a golden opportunity to improve your situation and you're not the least bit grateful."

Unable to find the right response, Phoena concentrated on calming her breathing. All manner of crazy thoughts whizzed through her head.

Finally, Heilga spoke again. "Come inside. You can't hide out here forever."

CHAPTER 3:
BEFORE DINNER

After lunch, Matron sent Phoena on an errand to the village which took most of the afternoon. The solitary walk gave her plenty of time to consider her situation. Yet no explanation or solution presented itself.

On the teenager's return, Heilga had summoned her to the dining hall. Dinner would be served in an hour. They were to prepare the tables for dinner. However, almost immediately after their arrival, Heilga disappeared. This was not an unusual occurrence – Phoena was accustomed to doing more than her share of the work.

She prowled around the room, making a final check that all the table settings were complete. The door reserved for the masters burst open. Matron and Headmaster Pepperbry entered, deep in conversation. The maid continued her work, but she could not avoid hearing every word.

"Trouble," Matron said. "I always knew there would be no other outcome. It was inevitable this girl would attract the wrong kind of attention."

"But we have the strongest protective spells in place," Headmaster Pepperbry replied. "These wards have always kept her talents hidden."

"Until today, I would have agreed with you, but Karilion has *noticed* her." Phoena became a silent statue at the mention of that young man's name. Matron continued, "And from what I saw at luncheon, he's not the only one."

"She was in the dining hall? Serving at Karilion's table? Was that wise?"

Matron looked at Phoena. The girl's heart jolted. The older woman's eyes flashed a silent warning for her to keep still. Matron frowned at him. "Headmaster, I had hoped you would recognise the problem for yourself. Perhaps the girl's

23

ability to make herself *invisible* is more effective than I realised. I brought you *here* to confirm my suspicions."

It was Headmaster Pepperbry's turn to frown. He scanned the room. Phoena trembled, but his eyes passed over her without acknowledgement. He shook his head. "You're always telling me that I can't see the problems immediately in front of me. What would you have me do?"

"The girl is blind to the powerful influences that surround her. I want permission to unveil her mind."

"Are you certain there's no other way?"

"Karilion has already tried a few charms, and she deflected them without effort. Can you predict the outcome if he discovers her real *potential*?"

"Is it that serious?"

"The Emberite Ambassador's son was *also* involved," Matron said.

Headmaster Pepperbry muttered something about an international incident and turned towards the door. He took three long strides before he spun back towards Matron. "Only her guardian can give the permission you seek. I forbid you to take any action until I have apprised him of the situation."

Without another word, the headmaster hurried from the room. Matron watched him leave. She nodded to Phoena, before following him through the same door.

When she was alone, the teenager dropped to her knees. She held her pounding head in her hands. The words she had overheard made no sense. Matron had never hinted that she knew anything about Phoena's origins. A whirlwind of possibilities threatened her sanity.

What was she to make of the headmaster's inability to see her? And what of this talk about "powerful influences"?

There was no possibility that Phoena had any powers. Indeed, *everyone* knew that Phoena was talentless. She was one of the few in this household who could not even discern magical use. She had only recently avoided disaster. A group of mischievous first-years had directed a spell at her on the stairs.

Afterwards, they confessed to practising some basic enchantments. They denied using anything powerful enough to throw her over the balcony. Witnesses said she flipped through the air as if she was flying. All she could remember was a loud bang, and then she was clinging to the banister railing with her feet dangling over the open stairwell. The students had sounded the alarm, and a passing footman had rescued her.

Heilga said she was unbelievably lucky. Either that or these students were lulling her into a false sense of security. Her friend warned her to watch out for the next trap.

What would Heilga make of this mysterious guardian who was to be consulted about her fate? Phoena shuddered. Her nights were often disturbed by strange dreams. Now her imagination ran riot. At the height of this insanity, she heard whirring dragon wings. The delusion was convincing. She shook her head. A daytime fantasy was worse than any nightmare.

Phoena refused to lift her head from her hands, and she scrunched her eyes shut. She ignored the persistent chirping from the imaginary dragonet, and the prickly sensation as if tiny talons dug into her shoulder. She even imagined that the phantom creature butted its head against her chin.

"Go away," she told it. "Torment someone else."

The fantasy hissed and then faded away.

Fifteen minutes before dinner, footmen entered the dining hall to draw the heavy curtains and light the candles. One of them threw her a curious glance as she struggled to her feet. She hurried from the room before anyone demanded an explanation. Weaving through the gathered crowd of servants, Phoena ran to the washroom. She stayed longer than she should.

Finally, she splashed cool water over her face and checked her reflection in the small wall mirror. Nothing she saw made her smile. That nose was too long. Those dishwater-grey eyes too wide apart. A wayward strand of mousy-brown hair was loose again. She tucked it into the knot at the nape of her neck. From the cupboard, she selected a pleated white headband and shoved it on.

The door flew open as Heilga stormed into the washroom. "The soup course is about to be served. I had to load the trolley myself, and now Matron is asking after you." Phoena smoothed her apron with her hands. She followed Heilga to the line of assembled trolleys.

"Table Two," Heilga said as she took her place. "It was costly persuading the other team to swap. So if you do anything to disappoint me, I'll never speak to you again."

CHAPTER 4:
KARILION'S WAGER

"I told you that she loved me," Lord Karilion cried when Heilga rolled the trolley to a stop beside him. Phoena ignored him as she ladled the rich beef broth into heated bowls.

"You have me to thank," Heilga said with a cheeky smile. "Fee would rather be serving the first-years. She didn't appreciate the way you teased her earlier."

"Fee, is that her name?" he asked. "Is it short for Fiona? Or Felicity?" Phoena shook her head, and he chuckled. "I'm sure I'll find *someone* who can tell me."

Phoena glared at her friend, as the twelve diners around the table began to laugh. She placed the soup bowl before Lord Karilion with a thump. Several drops of thick reddish broth splashed onto the white tablecloth. When she blanched at her mistake, Karilion moved the bowl to cover the stain.

"I don't like to see you displeased with me," he said. He waved his hand in the air. Did she imagine that sparkling twinkle at his fingertips? There was no ignoring the pink flower that magically appeared a few seconds later.

"Please accept this token as my apology."

Phoena accepted the delicate bloom with reluctance. The flower didn't seem real, and her skin tingled where she held the stem. Her fingers grew hot, and she gasped. The flower dropped to the table, where it burst into a shower of sparks and vanished. Silence fell over the diners.

"Your apology had no substance," the teenager said as she moved on to serve the next nobleman. Phoena blocked her ears to any further comment. She continued her work as if nothing significant had occurred.

However, her mind screamed in alarm.

"Well played," Heilga said as they loaded the trolley for the fish course. "That was a good move, not revealing your true name. That captured his attention. Magicians highly value that kind of personal information. But I suspect you already knew that, because you've been secretive about it. He won't rest until he finds out what it is. Look, he's waving for you now."

"You go," Phoena said, dropping a serving spoon, and storming off to the kitchen to replace it.

Her friend had not returned when Phoena resumed her position near the trolley. Heilga was engaged in whispered conversation with Karilion. The other servants were watching that discussion. Phoena declined to ask, but upon her return, Heilga didn't hesitate in sharing her news.

"He asked what he'd done to offend you," Heilga said with a smile. "I assured him you were unaccustomed to being addressed by such an *honourable* gentleman. You didn't know the appropriate way to respond.

"Then I explained that you misunderstood his intentions because you'd been the victim of too many first-year pranks. I assured him that I would personally see to your education. If he would extend you a little patience, I could guarantee a better outcome. He thanked me for my assistance."

Heilga opened her fingers and brandished a silver coin. "He promised me another shilling if I persuaded you to meet him in the courtyard after dinner."

"I'm not meeting him anywhere."

Heilga laughed. "I made him no promises. Look, Matron's signalling for service to begin. I can't wait to see what he tries next."

"I'm not serving him." Phoena grabbed Heilga's end of the trolley. "You like him so much, you deal with him."

Heilga grinned, offering no resistance. The significance of the reversed roles was discussed around the table. Phoena maintained a calm silence until she turned the corner. Now she faced the dark youth who had assaulted her that morning. He reached for her hand after she set down his plate. Phoena hesitated, staring at her fingers imprisoned in his grasp.

He nodded. "It is only right that you frown at me. I behaved like a fool when I met you this morning." He still held her hand and wouldn't release her. He was shorter than she remembered. There was an impish quality about him, reminiscent of the younger students. He pushed back his chair and dropped into a low bow. "I am truly sorry," he said and bent over her hand to kiss it lightly. "Viscount Baraapa of Larimore, at your service."

A rousing cheer went up among the other diners. As she stepped back, he added, "I'm publically declaring my interest. I'm challenging both Karilion and Oramis for the right to pursue you."

In a daze, Phoena finished her duties. Could the situation get any worse? Heilga hustled her back to the kitchen where the teenager refused to budge from the trolley. Heilga was kept busy answering calls to assist at their table. Viscount Baraapa's challenge had inspired the other fourth-years to declare their intentions.

The stack of gold coins in the centre of the table could be seen from where she stood. Requests for more wine, fresh table napkins, even another pepper shaker. Heilga had many opportunities to entertain their fellow-servants with outrageous gossip.

Finally, Phoena could take no more. She stepped out of formation, intending to ask Matron to excuse her. But even as she summoned the courage to advance, Matron glared at her. The stern overseer's displeasure was obvious. As was the impatient hand gesture.

Obediently returning to her place, the teenager bit her lip and pressed against the wall, with her head bowed. All she could do now was pray for strength.

Phoena's face was ashen when the trolley was ready with the next course. She dreaded Matron's signal to deliver the roast venison to her tormentors. The bell rang. Heilga set the trolley in motion, forcing Phoena to walk backwards to her doom. Each painful step delivered her closer to the table. She picked up the first plate.

Lord Karilion was waiting. He watched her place the dish before him and then spoke. "You seem to be fading, my dear," he said. He boldly reached for her chin, tipping it towards him. "I only want to see you smile. What can I do to persuade you that I mean you no harm?"

Phoena didn't answer. As she turned away, he caught hold of her arm. She hesitated, staring at those fingers encircling her wrist. "Let me go."

He complied immediately. She stepped back to the trolley. A tingling sensation that had begun with his touch was impossible to banish. She reached out to place the next meal on the table. A glowing strand of azure light spiralled around her wrist. As she gaped at it, the light twisted into a blue metal bangle that sparkled in the candlelight.

"I don't want your trinkets," she exclaimed in dismay. Lord Karilion arose. His eyes locked on her arm. She attempted to shake the bangle loose. It seemed to be a perfect fit, too small to slip over her hand. He reached for her.

"No!" She backed away. This brought her against the masters' raised platform. Too late, she remembered the dining hall layout.

"What is the meaning of this?" Headmaster Pepperbry asked. Phoena spun around, but he wasn't looking at her. Instead, his glare was directed at Karilion.

The young man seemed unrepentant. He grinned as he stood beside her. "I am attempting to apologise to this maid for a minor inconvenience."

Finally, the older man rested his eyes on her. "It would seem that she does not welcome your attention. Girl, if this gift offends you, take it off immediately and give it back to him."

There was power behind his words that rocked Phoena to the core. Flashes of hot and cold ran through her body. Her heart raced even faster. She swayed on her feet. Karilion moved as if to catch her, but Phoena recovered her balance and stepped out of his reach.

"Take it back," she said, plucking at the metal band with her fingers. At first, the metal bangle resisted her attempts. Then it shimmered and flashed into an insubstantial strand of blue light. She twitched her fingers and tossed the object back to him. Karilion's eyes widened, and he did not attempt to catch it. His smile faded as it fizzed into oblivion. He looked from Phoena to Headmaster Pepperbry and bowed low.

"There is a puzzle here," Karilion muttered as he retreated to his table.

"What is your name, girl?" one of the other masters asked. Phoena flinched.

"Her name is not important," Matron said, appearing beside her. "She has work to do."

Phoena hurried back to her table. Matron remained beside her. A hush fell over the assembled noblemen. Under that intimidating woman's stern gaze, Phoena continued to place meals on the table. Their superior accompanied the pair of maids to the kitchen.

Heilga was quiet and said nothing until Matron had withdrawn. "When that blue band appeared on your wrist, there was an outcry from the other noblemen. Karilion had accepted their wagers and then resorted to cheating. How did you break his compelling spell?"

Phoena shrugged. "I don't know anything about a 'compelling spell'. Suddenly there was a bangle on my wrist. The headmaster ordered me to remove it. I only did as I was told."

Heilga narrowed her eyes. "I'm sure there's more to your story. Why are you keeping secrets from me?"

Matron saved Phoena from having to answer. "Fee, I want you out of sight for the duration of the meal. Go to the Infirmary and remain there until I summon you. I am sending a footman with you to make sure you get to the Infirmary without any further distractions."

The footman carried a message for Nurse to make sure this maid was gainfully employed. The other Infirmary servants were quick to find her a myriad of menial tasks.

CHAPTER 5:
AFTER DINNER DRAMA

Instead of the expected summons from Matron, a message arrived for the maid to remain in the Infirmary. Phoena was begrudgingly included in the evening meal that was served there. She had little appetite. Finally, Nurse ordered the unwanted teenager to retire to her room.

It was an hour earlier than she usually retired, and when she arrived, the dormitory was empty. She shared the small room with Heilga and two other maids. Phoena prepared for bed. Under the covers, she closed her eyes and prayed for sleep to come. She had a throbbing pain at her temples and was still awake when her roommates arrived. The teenager hoped the others would ignore her.

Heilga threw back the covers. "Don't pretend you're asleep." The older maid dropped onto the edge of the bed and grabbed Phoena by the shoulders. "Not even you could sleep after all that excitement."

Phoena sighed and rolled over to face Heilga. A knock sounded at the door, and the room filled with other maids.

They gathered around her bed, whispering with excitement. She sat up with trepidation.

"You must be curious," Heilga insisted, "about what happened when you didn't reappear. Matron forbade me to say anything to the young men about where you were sent. Of course, I was careful to repeat that prohibition. That incited the fourth-years to offer me bribes to bring them whatever news I could discover."

Heilga brought her hands from her pockets. "I am to send word to the young noblemen, with anyone who can get past Matron..." Gold and silver coins rained onto the bed. "Of course, those messengers will also be rewarded."

Phoena began to protest, but Heilga silenced her with a wave. "We'll tell them that you've taken us into your confidence. *We* will speak on your behalf."

A chorus of agreement swept through the room.

"The first message must include an affirmation," Heilga

33

said. "You are grateful for the interest shown by every one of them. Of course, you must persuade them that you are open to all offers. We have discussed how we should proceed..." There was something sinister in the way Heilga was smiling at her. "A few locks of your hair will be an appropriate sacrifice."

Phoena lurched backwards. Merciless hands grabbed hold of her. Someone ripped the nightcap from her head. Another girl produced a pair of scissors.

The teenager struggled, but her attackers outnumbered her. When they finally released her, she raised her hand to assess the damage. Her hair had been her only redeeming feature.

Now, it was so short there was nothing to tuck into her nightcap.

Phoena fought back tears at this cruel betrayal. "I thought you were my friend."

The older maid shoved the cap over the shorn head. "You will thank me when you reap the rewards. Your hair will grow soon enough. Each of the young lords will sleep happier, believing you have given them a personal memento."

The locks of hair were dispatched under Heilga's instructions.

After the room emptied, Phoena pulled the covers over her head and turned towards the wall. She lay awake into the early morning hours, heartbroken and anxious about what was to come.

Dawn was breaking when Phoena crept from the bedroom. She carried her day clothes with her. The girl tiptoed to the washroom at the end of the hallway. After she dressed, she splashed cold water on her face. She didn't spare more than a glance in the mirror at her short hair.

The ragged style was not dissimilar to that worn by the urchins who swept the chimneys.

Phoena stealthily negotiated the dim hallways until she came to Matron's office. With a sigh, the teenager sat on the floor with her back against the locked door, wrapping her arms around her legs. Her eyes closed in prayer.

Phoena drifted into a troubled sleep. Her dreams were worse than usual. Fluttering dragon wings pursued her through endless hallways. Glowing bands of magical light tried to trap her. Young men chased her, making impossible demands.

She was rudely awoken an hour later.

"Fee, what are you doing here?" Matron demanded, pulling Phoena to her feet. "You should have stayed within the confines of your room, where you are protected."

Matron unlocked the door and dragged the maid into the office. The door closed with a bang. "Why are you wearing your nightcap outside your bedroom?" The cap lifted from her head. A stunned silence followed.

"So that's how the game has proceeded," Matron muttered, examining Phoena's new hairstyle. "Don't those fools understand the mischief they've unleashed by passing out your hair to so many magic users? It is just as well they don't know your true name, or this trouble would be multiplied."

Phoena's eyes opened wider. Her lips trembled as she fought the gathering emotional storm. Her ignorance regarding magical intrigue was greater than she imagined. "Please send me away."

"I'll do no such thing. You wouldn't last five minutes out in the open. We haven't kept you hidden here for fourteen years to have you lost at the first hint of controversy."

"Then send me back to the scullery."

"That option is closed to you," Matron said "We kept you there until the risk became too great. As an orphaned scullery maid, you were ripe for abuse by anyone. They had no fear of retribution.

"We had protective wards in place to protect you, but this brought an unexpected problem. Cook realised your innocence would bring him an excellent price. Only his greed delayed your arranged marriage to one of the tradesmen. As soon as our spies brought us that information, we removed you from his influence."

"I don't understand why you care what happens to an orphan," Phoena said. "Whether I'm sold to a tradesman or won in a nobleman's wager, the outcome is the same."

"You will have answers soon enough," Matron promised, softening her tone. "But for now, let us see what we can do to repair the damage already done to your reputation. By their greed, those servants have proclaimed you too willing to play the *wrong* game."

The austere woman rang a bell to summon a footman. The uniformed man eyed Phoena with curiosity. Next, Matron selected a pile of blank message cards. These were the kind used for correspondence between staff and students. Matron spread them across her desk. She waved her hand and began to speak. "Last evening–"

As Phoena watched, shiny magical threads swirled in the air. A group of feathered quills rose in unison from a large inkpot. Each one began to write Matron's spoken words onto a card in an identical, dainty script. Matron paused, smiling at Phoena's fascination, before she continued.

"–an innocent girl was robbed of her hair. The stolen hair was distributed with false promises. An amnesty is extended to each unwitting recipient of this deception. Signed Matron,"

The quills flew back to the inkpot. Matron turned to an open ledger on her desk. Her hand swept down a column of names.

"Table Two," Matron said, as she nominated a single quill. When she read aloud from the list, the name of each nobleman from that table appeared at the top of a card.

She continued until each card bore a name. Matron brought the cards together in a stack and passed them to the footman. Then she selected a larger piece of parchment and dictated a notice.

"There is a reward of two shillings for information about the theft and distribution of hair. Amnesty is available to anyone who confesses their involvement before midday. Failure to come forward will result in instant dismissal. This will include the forfeiture of any outstanding wages and entitlements."

When Matron had finished, she sent the quill back to the inkwell. Finally, she addressed the footman. "This notice must be displayed in the servants' dining room, beside the daily roster."

The footman received the parchment with a bow and spun on his heels. He left the room without a word.

Matron paused in thought. She opened a drawer and brought out a silver comb. Phoena knelt as she was directed, and closed her eyes.

Matron drew the comb through Phoena's hair while she hummed an unfamiliar tune. The girl's head tingled, and she wondered what was happening. When Matron finished humming, Phoena opened her eyes in time to see the silver comb returning to its home. And then Matron pulled out a scrap of white lace. Phoena caught a glimpse of brilliant light, and felt pressure on the top of her head. The older woman held an oval mirror in an ornate gilded frame in front of Phoena.

The maid's eyes grew wide. What remained of her hair now ended with dainty curls which peeked out from under an unusual cap. This style gave the illusion that the rest of her hair was concealed.

Matron smiled and instructed Phoena to stand. She asked the maid to remove her white apron and then wrapped a shawl around her shoulders. "At first glance, you will pass as a visiting lady's maid. It is fortunate that this misadventure has taken place at the start of the semester. There are still some anxious mothers staying here."

Now, she opened another drawer and brought out a rectangular object, the size and shape of a cake of soap, but the smooth surface was warm to touch. Matron passed it to Phoena. "The only thing that can erase magical ink is a magical eraser. Take yourself the roundabout way to the servants' dining room, and be careful not to speak to anyone. That will break the illusion. When you reach the dining room, locate your name on the roster. Memorise your assignment for today, and then wave this eraser over your name. It is tuned to my writing. When your name has been removed, return to me without delay."

Phoena slipped the white eraser into her pocket and followed Matron's instructions. As she tiptoed through the empty corridors, she puzzled over why she had been sent back into public view. The only reason that made any sense was that Matron didn't want her to know what Matron was doing now.

With great relief, the maid arrived in the dining room, undetected by other servants. The room was empty. Matron's notice was already pinned to the noticeboard.

Phoena turned to the roster and looked for her name. She was not assigned to any of the students' or masters' bedrooms, nor was her name allocated to the dining hall. A quick search of the classroom list and the other public spaces was unproductive.

Panic was nibbling at her resolve by the time she finally found what she was looking for: "Fee". She had been assigned to the ground floor guest apartments in the northern wing of the school. These suites were reserved for members of the King's Council and rarely used. The list of tasks was long and her name was the only one assigned. Phoena sighed and brought out the eraser. She waved the eraser over the name that everyone here knew her by, and waited.

A swirl of light flashed between her hand and the roster. Then a trail of purple text lifted from the parchment and drifted outward. After the ink had vanished into the eraser, Phoena examined the white object. There was no blemish on the pristine surface. She slipped the eraser back into her pocket and turned for the door.

At that moment, some of the maids involved in last night's incident arrived. Phoena lowered her eyes and shouldered her way past them. She ignored their complaints and hurried along the passage. A few seconds later, she heard a cry of outrage behind her – they must be reading the notice! Her feet took flight.

She narrowly avoided a collision with a group of younger

students in a connecting hallway. Only when she arrived at the door to Matron's office did the maid pause. After smoothing her skirts, Phoena knocked on the door.

Matron responded quickly, ushering her in. The maid placed the eraser in Matron's outstretched hand and awaited further instructions.

"Sit over there." Matron pointed to a chair in the corner. She gave Phoena the gilded mirror again and turned back to her desk.

Phoena sat in silence, resisting the temptation to gaze into the mirror, and finding it increasingly difficult to stay awake. As she dozed, she heard the sound of angry voices. Startled, she looked for the visitors and discovered that the noise was coming from the mirror. Vibrant colours swirled on the shiny surface. A few moments later, the colours faded. She must be having another hallucination. How else would she be able to see those familiar servants in their dining room?

The scene was so realistic it felt as if she was there beside them. Heilga was standing at the noticeboard, surrounded by the other maids.

Heilga ripped the notice about the stolen hair from the noticeboard. "We all know Fee is too timid to tell anyone what we did. She's hiding somewhere, and she'll reappear when she's hungry."

"How did Matron find out?" several maids asked at once.

Heilga shrugged. "One of the noblemen must have been caught with her hair. Without Fee's testimony, there's nothing to worry about. If we stand together and keep quiet, we'll be safe."

"*You* will be safe," another woman muttered. "The rest of us were the messengers. When the students find out the hair was stolen, they'll be quick to identify us. I vote that we go to Matron and confess. I don't want to be dismissed."

"You've seen enough," Matron said, snatching away the mirror. She silenced the image with a wave of her hand.

There came a knock at the door, and the same footman entered. This time he carried a covered tray. He placed it on a small table, bowed to Matron and backed from the room.

"A good servant doesn't need instruction," Matron said with a smile, "to understand what is required. You must have a hearty breakfast before I banish you to the northern wing."

Matron lifted the lid. Phoena stared at the mound of bacon, sausages and poached eggs, and the thick slices of hot buttered toast. There were enough plates and cutlery for two. Matron passed a plate to Phoena, before serving herself and beginning to eat. Phoena's stomach rumbled as she chose sparingly. The girl chewed each mouthful in slow appreciation. How different this meal was from her usual breakfast – watery porridge, eaten in haste before someone sent her on an errand. Matron ate heartily, pausing only to add more food to Phoena's plate.

"You're too thin," Matron said. "I couldn't do anything to make life easier for you without giving away too much. But the time for caution is long past."

When Phoena could not eat another morsel, Matron gathered the plates. Then she handed Phoena an apron before leading the maid to the bookcase on the far wall. Matron examined the books on the middle shelf and selected one. With a swirl of light, a magical doorway appeared where the bookcase had been.

Matron ushered Phoena towards the spiralling portal. "I don't want anyone to know where you're hiding."

The maid hesitated. "Obey me," Matron said, "and all will be well." The teenager stumbled through the portal. As the office disappeared, she heard Matron speak again. "Phoena, unlock the courage inside you."

Alone in the hallway of the guest wing, the teenager looked around. There was no sign of the door through which she had entered. She spun on her heels. How had she come here? But there was a deeper question she pushed down into the depths of her heart. Phoena had never told anyone what the voices in her dreams called her, yet Matron knew her name!

CHAPTER 6:
BANISHED TO THE GUEST WING

Three hours later, Phoena was halfway through the assigned tasks. She had put on her familiar apron but removed the delicate lace cap, fearing she might ruin it. The guest apartments had been dusted and aired in preparation for visitors.

A fresh fire burned in each fireplace to take away the chill that lingered in the seldom-used rooms. Now she must scrub the granite flagstones in the long hallway. She filled her bucket with water warmed in a kettle over one of the fires.

Phoena carried the bucket to the hallway. A stiff scrubbing brush and a large cake of harsh soap sat in readiness on the flagstones.

Her introduction to life outside the scullery had been strenuous – long hours dedicated to scrubbing the student hallways. Her body fell into a familiar rhythm. She began at the huge doorway that led to the garden. Crawling backwards, she scrubbed. The repetitive movement of her arms freed her mind to reflect on recent events.

The teenager refused to speculate over Matron's motivation. She also shut down thoughts about Heilga's betrayal. But try as she might, she couldn't stop thinking about the fourth-year students.

Her predictable life had changed after that first encounter with the dragonet. She envied the little monster its freedom. These feelings must be potent, because they continued to inspire hallucinations. Her aching arms assured her that she was awake.

So why did she imagine she could hear the sound of delicate wings nearby? She glanced around, but could see no evidence that the noise was real. There was no magical creature here.

Phoena bent back to her scrubbing, unable to shake a prickly sensation across her shoulders. As the minutes passed, a certainty grew that she was no longer alone. Phoena looked again and listened carefully. Was that a flurry of dark shadows halfway along the hallway? She held her breath. The silence throbbed in her ears. Nothing moved.

Her scrubbing continued for another five minutes. This time, it was the sound of footsteps she imagined in front of her. She lifted her head. A red flash drew her attention to a darkened doorway. Was that a door opening? Then a pillar of swirling shadow resolved itself into the shape of a man.

"Who's there?" Phoena asked.

The blond nobleman, Lord Oramis, stepped forward with a smile. "I came to make sure you were safe. I received Matron's note about your stolen hair. She was unhelpful when I asked her to explain how you fared after that ordeal."

"You can see," Phoena said, resuming her scrubbing, "that the loss of my hair did nothing to keep me from my chores. Nor has it robbed me of my strength. You should go, unless you want me to be accused of neglecting my work."

"I'll rest here a while to determine for myself whether you have been robbed of your strength."

To match his words, he chose one of the carved chairs that stood at regular intervals between the framed portraits along the wood-panelled hall. He sat between the portrait of the old king and the current one. She had already dusted all the portraits and knew they had been painted long ago.

"Here's a pretty scene," another voice declared. Phoena bumped the bucket in surprise, and water sloshed across the floor.

"What are you doing here?" Oramis hissed, rising to his feet.

"I came looking for you, Oramis," Lord Karilion replied. "I had no success finding our maid. Her hair didn't work for my seeking spell. So when I learned of your interview with Matron, I sought you instead."

After mopping the spill, Phoena turned her attention to the two young men standing in her hallway. Karilion's boots were muddy. "Look at the mess you've made of my floor!" she wailed, reaching for her scrubbing brush. Then she blinked. The trail of footprints did not come from the doorway. Instead, they emerged from the wall. "How did you walk through that wall?"

Karilion studied the rest of the damp floor. "You should be asking the same question about Oramis. His tracks lead from an internal doorway."

At that moment, the main door leading from the garden burst open. Three more noblemen rushed in.

"Stop!" Phoena shouted, leaping to her feet. "This hallway is out of bounds. I've just scrubbed that floor, and I don't have time to do it again."

"We'll take off our boots," Viscount Baraapa assured her. His companions followed his example. They were the same friends who had been involved in ransacking Karilion's room. She had never seen the Viscount without them.

They dropped their boots at the entrance and walked across her floor in stockinged feet. Phoena threw up her hands in dismay. "I have work to do," she said. She devoted herself to the task with renewed energy. She prayed that they would all tire of watching her work and go away.

"I see you both found her," Baraapa said. "When neither of you were in any of the public spaces, I knew you must be with her. We didn't have your magical advantage, and relied on scientific logic instead."

"And how did logic help?" Karilion asked.

"We sneaked into the servants' dining room and checked the roster."

"So did I," Karilion said. "Her name wasn't listed anywhere."

"It wasn't a question of finding her name," Baraapa said, "but looking for space where a name used to be."

"Should I worry because that makes sense?" Oramis asked.

Karilion spun towards him. "You haven't explained how you found her."

"I did it the old fashioned way. I sent the first-year students out as spies. I promised them a week's supply of sweets if they reported back to me within the half-hour. When they found no sign of her, I knew she had to be in one of the restricted areas."

The floor under Phoena's knees rumbled. She sat up, looking around with concern.

"Something's coming," Baraapa said.

Karilion frowned. "It must be powerful if even a non-magic like you can sense it."

Wave after wave of white light pulsated along the hallway. A glowing spiral appeared on the wall. A portrait of the previous headmaster had hung there moments earlier. Phoena continued scrubbing but kept her head up. She watched with wide eyes.

"We can't be found here!" The most recent arrivals raced back the way they had come. There were shouts of frustration. "The door is locked!"

"Karilion," Baraapa cried, running back with his boots in his hands. His companions were a few steps behind him. "Can you transport us out of here?"

"It's too late," Karilion said. "I've already tried to leave, and it can't be done. I was able to break through the basic defences to get in here, but now there's a new kind of barrier. I've not encountered anything like it. It surrounds the whole wing. I can't find a weakness. It looks as if we're stuck here. I recommend we prepare ourselves to meet whoever, or whatever, is coming."

Oramis stepped closer to Phoena and extended his hand. "Allow me to offer you my protection."

She shook her head. "There's no danger for me. I'm supposed to be here." She bowed to her task, determined not to let him see her fear. Her hands kept scrubbing.

An uneasy stillness fell over the young men. The pulsating light expanded outward, to become a bright circle in the centre of the hallway.

The circle floated closer, growing until it spanned the wide space from floor to ceiling. Three robed figures appeared within the light, walking towards them. The brightness behind these figures made it difficult to make out their features.

But the one in the middle was a giant, half as tall again and twice as wide as his companions. He carried a long staff.

It took all of Phoena's stubborn determination to keep her hands moving. The sound of the abrasive brush echoed in her ears. From her low vantage point, she watched three pairs of boots step from the brightness onto her damp floor. The young noblemen retreated from view. She could hear them muttering somewhere behind her.

The visitors continued to approach. When they were only an arms-length away, all three stopped. The giant tapped his staff on the floor. The portal behind him disappeared with a loud whoosh.

Phoena blinked as her eyes readjusted to the normal light. She recognised the smaller figures. The tall woman was Matron. The second man was Headmaster Pepperbry. Neither school official was smiling.

Careful to keep her head bowed, Phoena peered at the giant through her lashes. The frowning man had bushy white hair and a long beard that came almost to the floor. He wore old-fashioned burgundy robes. The staff in his hand was topped with a carved silver ornament. He was dressed in the same style as the man in the portrait that hung on the wall behind him. She looked a second time.

He *was* the man in the portrait.

There was a legend beside that portrait. Her memory provided her with additional information. This giant was both the founder of the school and the previous headmaster. She swallowed her fear and put more energy into her scrubbing.

Phoena prayed that he would overlook her presence.

"I wasn't expecting a welcoming committee," the bearded giant said in a booming voice.

"One wasn't prepared, Lord Westernbrooke," the current headmaster said with a frown. "What are—"

Lord Westernbrooke waved his staff impatiently. "Introductions, first, Pepperbry. Explanations will follow – if required."

"Lord Karilion of Hemington." The young lord stepped forward. Phoena admired his courage.

"I remember your father," Lord Westernbrooke replied. "He was one of our more promising students. Such a tragedy that he died young, but he was always a reckless boy. I'm not surprised to find his heir involved in mischief here at the *Academy.*" The imposing giant huffed. "Although, I had hoped Pepperbry could instil some common sense in you before your political debut. You turn eighteen next month, and that entitles you to your father's seat on the King's Council."

Karilion bowed again.

The blond youth stepped forward with a bow. His black clothes seemed understated beside the more ornate costume of his rival. "Lord Oramis, son of Draggo Oramis, the Emberite Ambassador to the King's Council." Oramis straightened and met the headmaster's glare with boldness. "At your service, Lord Westernbrooke. My father, you may also remember. But perhaps for reasons which need not be mentioned in *this* company."

Phoena puzzled over this latter remark, certain that Oramis had gestured towards her. Why would the presence of a maidservant have any significance in this conversation?

"Indeed," Lord Westernbrooke said. "I will reserve my opinion until I have met the remaining companions."

"Viscount Baraapa of Larimore, and my two men-at-arms: Virago of Grandeheill and his younger brother, Virtuo."

"Younger by only five minutes," Virtuo muttered. "And we're only here because the Viscount dragged us along."

"That's not what you said at dinner last night," Karilion remarked, "when you offered your names for the challenge."

"Ah!" Lord Westernbrooke said. "The challenge."

He turned towards Phoena and knocked the scrubbing brush from her hand with his staff. "If you don't stop scrubbing that stone, child, you will wear out my floor. Stand up!"

Phoena scrambled to her feet. She dropped into a low curtsey, keeping her eyes downcast. The shaft of the staff appeared below her chin. Lord Westernbrooke used it to encourage her to look into his eyes. He didn't seem pleased. The girl blushed. He turned towards Matron and raised an eyebrow.

Karilion stepped forward in her defence. "Fee is innocent. She wanted no part in any of this." The other young men echoed their agreement.

Lord Westernbrooke silenced them with his hand. He turned to Matron. "I ordered you to keep her in isolation until I arrived. How did these *boys* make it past your security?"

Matron stiffened, yet met his eyes without hesitation. "Cousin, you already know that two of them are magicians of the highest order. The blond foreigner shape-shifted past my defences."

The other students cried out in surprise, and Headmaster Pepperbry frowned.

"When Karilion scented the trail," Matron continued, "he used his rival's coordinates to transport himself in. And the Viscount is clever and persistent – he enjoys a challenging hunt."

Lord Westernbrooke studied them anew, before turning back to Matron. "And how did the girl become the quarry in this hunt?"

"Ask them yourself. But if this is a formal interrogation, move it somewhere comfortable." The older woman propelled Phoena towards the closest doors which flew open at their approach. "The girl has already lit the fires in preparation for your arrival."

Matron swept into the reception room with the trembling maid trailing in her wake.

Although the curtains were open, it was unnaturally dark in the room. Phoena glanced at the windows. The colour drained from her face. Instead of landscaped gardens, the panes revealed only a midnight-blue haze. Matron appeared unconcerned, raising her hand. Candles ignited, and the room brightened. Matron nodded towards the fireplace. Phoena hurried to stir the coals and add more fuel to the fire.

Matron settled on one of the low padded sofas. "We shall have tea." She directed the men towards the other seats arranged around an ornate table. Lord Westernbrooke took up a whole sofa.

Phoena blinked. Only once had she been present for a tea ceremony. Last year, she had helped prepare refreshments in a humbler apartment. On that occasion, one of the visiting lady's maids had laid out the necessities. As the only servant present today, Phoena would have to perform that role. With a shaking hand, she reached for the kettle. After confirming it was full, she swung it over the flames.

Snatches of conversation drifted towards her. The Viscount spoke first. "...chasing Oramis... Karilion's apartment..."

Phoena assembled the tea-making things. She selected delicate china cups and placed them on a tray.

"...she denied that she'd seen him... impossible..."

After placing lumps of sugar in a bowl, Phoena filled a crystal jug with chilled milk.

She berated herself for not questioning earlier why these fresh provisions were here.

"...didn't know about *his* magic..."

Shaking her head, Phoena tried to process the new information. Matron had said the blond Lord was a shape-shifter. The clues fell into place. The disembodied voice; the sudden appearance of the dragonet. The dragon brooch should have been a warning to her.

As if her thoughts were directing the interview, Oramis began to speak. "I didn't let her see me..."

Phoena searched the cupboards for other provisions. She didn't want to hear him reveal what happened in the garden. She found a covered box filled with sugar-dusted shortbread. Another box held a selection of chocolates. These treats she arranged on a two-tiered stand.

When the tray was ready, Phoena placed it on the table before Matron, who nodded her approval. "Bring one more cup, when you return with the teapot."

There were four varieties of dried leaves in the wooden tea caddy. Phoena chewed her lip and spooned some of each kind into the crystal mixing bowl. She would have to guess the right proportions to make a fragrant herbal brew.

She stirred the leaves with a silver spoon and then added the tea to the infuser. With care, she poured boiling water from the kettle into the massive teapot. The lid snapped into place. With the extra cup nestled beside the teapot, Phoena carried the second tray to the table. She curtsied and prepared to back away.

Matron touched her arm. "Sit here, and pour."

Phoena blinked and fought the desire to run away. Why would Matron ask a lowly chambermaid to play the role of hostess? She sank onto the sofa beside Matron. Her heart skipped.

With trembling hands, the teenager poured milk into the first cup, added steaming liquid from the teapot, and reached for the sugar tongs. "One lump or two?" she asked, lifting her eyes to Lord Westernbrooke. She marshalled her face into what she hoped was a polite smile.

"No sugar," the intimidating gentleman said.

Phoena passed him the cup. The process was repeated with the other dignitaries. Headmaster Pepperbry took three sugars, Matron only one. Lord Karilion, Viscount Baraapa and the twins each requested two sugars. Lord Oramis took his tea with neither milk nor sugar. Phoena laid her hands in her lap when she had finished.

"Don't forget a cup of tea for yourself," Matron said.

Phoena looked at her in alarm. Matron handed the teenager the spare cup, and she added milk and tea. Phoena sat stiffly, her eyes focused on the liquid while she carefully balanced the cup on the saucer. The older woman passed around the tiered plate of dainty treats. The maid dimly noted the polite conversation.

Finally, Phoena brought the cup to her lips and took a small sip. Her throat felt tight, making it impossible to swallow. She choked back a small cough. Now would be a good time to be invisible, she thought, praying the floor would open up and consume her. The room began to fade.

"Careful!" Matron cried.

Phoena's fingers were tingling. Her hands lost hold of the saucer as the dainty cup tipped sideways. The cup hit the edge of the table and exploded into pieces. Broken china and spilt liquid flew in every direction.

At the same time, Phoena's body was being pulled and stretched along with it. She threw a terrified glance towards Matron, as the pain became unbearable.

Swirling darkness opened beneath Phoena's feet. "Oh!"

Before the maid could say anything else, she fell into the vortex. The last thing she remembered was something hot and fierce thumping against her. The heat wrapped itself around her.

CHAPTER 7:
UNDERGROUND

Phoena lay still as darkness pressed against her.

She must be wrapped in a thick, warm blanket. She could feel the beating of her heart, so strong and loud that it seemed to be coming from outside her body.

Carefully, she lifted her head.

The blanket moved. There were two hearts beating. Her own now thumped rapidly in her chest, while the second one pounded beside her. She was enveloped in the embrace of a living creature.

She pushed herself away and tumbled onto the hard ground.

High above, a pair of glowing red eyes tracked her movement. Phoena crept backwards on her haunches until she encountered a cold, hard barrier. A rock wall. She was in the monster's lair.

Mindless terror stole her reason. Not a sound passed her lips. No fragment of prayer flew heavenward.

The red eyes closed, leaving her trembling in the dreadful darkness.

A stone clattered beside her. Was the monster about to devour her?

Before she could react, something hot and scaly began winding itself around her chest. Phoena tried to scramble to her feet while pushing and pulling at the binding thing.

It tightened until she could no longer breathe. Her strength failed, and she sagged to the ground.

When she came to her senses, the hot tightness confirmed her captivity.

"What do you want with me?" she asked the darkness.

The pair of red eyes opened above her, no closer than they had been before.

"Can you speak?" Phoena asked.

The creature responded with a terrifying roar. The air above her ignited. The looming outline of a glistening dragon appeared through the smoke. A moment later, the flames died. Only the red eyes remained to relieve the darkness.

That brightness had been enough for her to recognise him. This was the dragon-lord, Oramis. She had wrestled with him as a tiny dragon. Now he was huge! Was this his way of repaying her for attempting to catch him in the back garden?

The maid touched the thing wrapped around her body. "Is this your tail?"

The dragon blinked. The binding twitched in response.

"Are you going to eat me?"

The eyes loomed closer. Winding coils of his tail dragged her forward, delivering her into the dragon's firm embrace. Phoena trembled between his forearms.

The red eyes floated nearer until she felt the intense heat of the monster's breath blowing over her face. For a moment, she feared that he would set her on fire.

When he didn't consume her, she breathed again. Phoena reached through the darkness and touched the dragon's snout with her hand. Her quivering fingers brushed against his skin. The dragon blinked. His snout pressed against her face with a gentleness that surprised her.

She withdrew her hand.

"I'm glad you don't want to eat me."

The dragon's head moved further away. His eyes half-closed and tilted sideways as if he was reconsidering the matter. A glimmering puff of smoke wafted towards her.

"Are you– are you... teasing me?"

Another puff of smoke was followed by the tiniest burst of flame.

"What? Do you think I'm teasing you? I wouldn't dare. I know my place."

Whoomph!

The dragon butted her chest with his snout before raising his head. Phoena puzzled over the unspoken question.

Finally, she said, "This is *not* my place!"

The dragon responded with a terrifying roar. The

darkness fled before the blazing brightness. Phoena shielded her eyes, peering through her fingers at the marvel. The heat was almost unbearable.

She shrank back against his chest. They must be magic flames – she was unharmed.

The beast roared until the flames reached the distant ceiling. They were in a rock-lined chamber. The cavern was almost as wide as the grand dining hall at the *Academy* – and twice as high.

Phoena sought a way out. She saw two exits, a smaller one on the further side, and a tunnel mouth a few paces away. When the dragon fell silent, the oppressive gloom reclaimed its dominance.

The dragon butted her chest again.

Red eyes stared into her own.

"How can this be my place? I've never been here before."

The dragon blew smoke at her again.

"Neither have you? But that shouldn't be a problem for you. You're a magical creature. You can fly out of here."

The dragon sent a burst of flame towards the closest tunnel.

Phoena puzzled over his response. "You're too large for the opening? But you can change your size. If you make yourself smaller, you can find your way out of here."

The tail around her waist tightened.

Phoena pushed at it with her hands. "Stop that. If you squeeze me too tight, I can't breathe."

The red eyes blinked, and the tail twitched twice. But the pressure eased.

"You're worried that I won't be able to follow you?"

The dragon's eyes closed, and the creature stilled its breathing.

Phoena puzzled over this response. He remained still for so long she feared that something bad had happened to the dragon-lord. She leaned against his chest and listened for his heartbeat. At that moment, a horrifying idea came to her.

"Oh! You're afraid that I'll close off the tunnel and trap you."

The dragon stared at her. Phoena rested her arms on the coiled tail and considered this revelation. She recalled the dark portal that had opened under her feet when she had prayed for the floor to consume her.

Phoena shook her head. "This is my fault? But how did you get here? You were seated—"

The dragon flapped his wings.

"You changed your shape and flew at me. Why would you do that?"

A puff of orange flame warmed her face. The dragon wrapped an arm around her and applied gentle pressure.

"You didn't want me to face the unknown without help. I am glad to have your company, My Lord. Why don't you change back into your human form? I need you to tell me what I have to do to get us out of here."

The dragon closed his eyes again.

Phoena sighed. "You still don't trust me."

CHAPTER 8:
AN
UNEASY
ALLIANCE

The dragon was asleep. Phoena waited in the darkness, listening to his heartbeat. Puffs of spark-laden smoke wafted upward from the snout that rested on her shoulder.

She had run out of declarations and petitions and could find no way out of her predicament. She was almost asleep when the dragon snorted and lifted his head. The red eyes turned towards the further tunnel.

Phoena listened. The sound of approaching footsteps grew louder. A glimmer of light revealed another presence. The dragon raised his coiled tail about her head, but Phoena pushed it lower until she could see.

Two shadowy figures stepped into the cavern. A glowing circle of light, the size of a small melon, floated at waist height in front of two men.

"How much longer are we going to wander in this maze of tunnels?" a familiar voice complained. What was Viscount Baraapa doing here? "I thought you said you could find Oramis."

The dragon roared and sent a blast of flame in their direction.

"And I have," Lord Karilion replied. He waved his hand, and the glowing orb that hovered before him grew larger. The two noblemen stared at the dragon, who narrowed his eyes.

Baraapa stepped forward without fear. "There's no need to show off, Oramis."

The dragon roared again. The two newcomers seemed undeterred.

"Where's the girl?" Baraapa demanded.

"Don't tell me you've lost her!" Karilion said.

"Of course he hasn't lost me." Phoena struggled to raise herself above the protective coils. "But I've failed to convince him that I won't run away. He thinks I might transport myself out again without taking him with me."

Baraapa and Karilion looked at each other.

Phoena moaned. "Don't tell me you're worried about that too?"

They shuffled their feet, and the dragon puffed smoke at her.

Phoena patted his neck and nodded. "Lord Oramis wants to know how you arrived here."

"You understand him?" Baraapa asked.

At the same time, Karilion muttered, "If you don't know how to lead us out of here, we're in trouble."

The dragon roared as if he was laughing.

"Matron said trouble follows me everywhere," Phoena said. "I know how Lord Oramis followed me. He saw the floor open beneath me, and he leapt at me as I fell. But I didn't sense your presence."

"We came a roundabout way," Karilion said. "I was watching for Oramis' shape-shifting magic. The portal closed so fast I almost missed my opportunity to activate a magical tracer."

"And I was stupid enough," Baraapa added, "to grab onto his cape as he leaned forward. He inadvertently dragged me along with him when he disappeared."

"When we were in the hallway, you said there was no way out," Phoena said. "So how do you explain what's happened to us?"

"I don't think we're out," Karilion replied. "You've brought us further in."

Phoena shook her head. "I don't know how to use magic."

The two noblemen laughed, and the dragon smoked her again.

"If you believe that, you're—" Karilion began.

Baraapa interrupted him. "We discussed the evidence while we were coming here. First, there's your ability to make yourself forgettable. I pride myself on my memory for faces and names, but I was certain I'd never seen you before I found you in Karilion's room. When I questioned the other servants, they told me you'd been here for years."

"You're not supposed to notice the servants," Phoena said.

"Notice you!" exclaimed Baraapa. "I find it hard to even focus on your face. Why do you think I grabbed hold of your arm in Karilion's room? I thought you were going to disappear. When I squint at you," Baraapa continued, "I'm almost convinced I can see what you truly look like."

"Active wards surround you," Karilion said. "Most ordinary mortals can't see them, but they're there if you know how to look for them. I recognised the deep magic as soon as I entered my room. I've tried different spells and been unable to penetrate your defences. The more powerful the spell, the greater your ability to deflect it."

"You've wounded his pride," Baraapa added. "You broke Karilion's spells as if he was an amateur. Everyone knows he's one of the most powerful magic users at the *Academy*. Yet you made defeating him look easy."

"I didn't know there were any spells," Phoena mumbled. Then she remembered the flashes of light she had seen. That had only begun after Matron asked for permission to unveil Phoena's eyes. Had Matron done something to her? Phoena frowned. What else was she unable to see?

The dragon nudged her.

"Have you wondered," Karilion asked. "Why our shape-shifting Emberite friend seems so determined to keep you close to him? Convenient that he forgot to tell anyone he was a dragon. Baraapa thinks Oramis was trying to find you when he broke into my room."

The dragon hissed at them and flapped his wings. He rose into the air until Phoena's feet no longer touched the ground.

"Let me go!" she cried. "You've already told me you're too big to fly out of here. I refuse to believe you would leave your friends behind."

Without warning, the dragon released the coils that bound her. Thankful that she had only a short distance to fall, Phoena tumbled across the ground. As she rolled, she wrapped her arms around her head to block out the terrible roar that filled the air. She crashed into the cavern wall.

The dragon rose in wide circles to the roof of the cave. He continued to roar until the cavern filled with smoke. The noise ended abruptly.

He had disappeared.

Phoena staggered to her feet.

"They are not my friends," Lord Oramis said, stepping out of the smoke in his human form. He stopped directly in front of Phoena. He wasn't smiling. "And I wasn't looking for you. I didn't know you existed. I thought I was dealing with an attack from a powerful sorcerer. Something had been hammering at my defences since I arrived at the *Academy*.

"I'm used to shielding myself from other magic users, but your power is something else. I tracked the source to Karilion's room, which surprised me. I'd been seated across from him at his table for two days, and sensed no threat."

Phoena glanced at the others. Karilion had his arms folded across his chest. Baraapa leaned forward with great interest. She returned her attention to Oramis.

"I walked up and down the hallway just to be sure. I was careful, but Baraapa must have seen me." Oramis glared at the smaller youth. "I thought they'd been led astray, but as I was unlocking Karilion's door, they appeared again."

Viscount Baraapa smiled.

"I had no choice," the dragon-lord continued, "but to shape-shift as soon as I entered the room. I was already in my dragon form when I saw you between me and the fireplace."

"You escaped through the fireplace?" Baraapa exclaimed.

Oramis turned towards him, which allowed Phoena space to step sideways.

"I only made it as far as the bucket she was carrying—"

"You were in the bucket?" Baraapa asked. "I didn't know shape-shifters could vary their size. You were a humungous dragon here. Are you able to withstand her power in your larger form?"

"If you want to hear my story," Oramis muttered, "don't interrupt me."

"I apologise," dark Baraapa replied, with a small bow. "Please continue, My Lord."

"You're very quick with your apologies." Oramis sneaked a glance towards Phoena. Everyone shuffled to return her to the centre of their circle.

"Baraapa," Oramis said, "your simple words have given you an advantage with our maiden. Far more than either Karilion or I have managed despite our magical scheming."

"Stop changing the subject," Karilion said. "Finish what you were saying."

"It was fortunate for me that she has an affinity for fire."

"What do you mean?" Karilion asked.

There was a pause. The corners of Oramis' mouth twitched. "If that ash bucket had contained water instead, I would have been soaked! I can assure you that soggy dragon smells worse than a wet dog."

"I'm sure there's something you're not telling us," Karilion muttered. "I want to know how you discovered her fire-affinity. But I can see that you don't intend to share that information. So I'll tell you what I've learned despite your deception."

Oramis smirked, but Karilion ignored him. The pair were well-matched in height and size. But the contrast between fair Oramis and dark-haired Karilion increased the drama.

"She couldn't recognise you in the dining hall," Karilion snarled, "because she didn't see your human form. She was captivated by the dragon brooch you were wearing. You boasted that you'd already won the challenge. But I can assure you it doesn't count if she *kissed* you while you were pretending to be a baby dragon."

"She's kissed him already?" Baraapa hissed.

"I have not!"

Oramis laughed at her denial. "She's not going to kiss a little monster who tried to set her on fire and then bit her. I think she might have tolerated me as a pet, given time to know me better. But any advantage my dragon form could bring me has now been lost."

He reached out and pushed Karilion. "I find it ironic that you accuse me of scheming for an unfair advantage. We all know you tried to magically coerce her."

Karilion's face flushed. "I've already explained – I was testing the limitations of her power." His hand slipped to where his sword should be if it hadn't been surrendered to the Armoury Master. The students were only permitted to carry their swords when they were away from school. He caught himself, but they all understood the gesture.

"You've changed the subject again," Karilion said. "You said you bit her! Do you have a death wish? She's dangerous."

"Dangerous!" Phoena spluttered, but they were lost to their argument.

"It was a test," Oramis said. "She had burnt her hand, and I was wondering how a fire-adept could come by such an injury. There is nothing like a little pain to–"

Phoena stomped her foot. "A little pain!"

Her words echoed through the cavern. An unfamiliar emotion flooded her mind while her hand acted without direction. With seconds to spare, she defeated the impulse to slap his face.

Instead, she covered her mouth with the offending hand and bowed her head.

She felt sick.

Torment must always be endured in silence. Despite years of abuse from her fellow servants, she had never openly protested. With her eyes closed, she edged further away.

Before she could begin her silent prayer of repentance, rough hands grabbed her.

"Don't let her get away!" Baraapa shouted. Phoena opened her eyes and pushed at his hands, but the small nobleman wouldn't release her.

Desperation made Baraapa strong. "If you leave me here, I have no magic to follow you."

She recognised the terror in his eyes. "I-I w-wasn't going anywhere."

He shook his head. "You were fading." In desperation, he turned to his companions.

Karilion nodded. "There was a surge of magical energy. If Baraapa hadn't moved, I would have lunged at you myself."

"Apart from wanting to hit me," Oramis said, "what was happening in your head?"

Phoena stared at Oramis.

Karilion nodded in understanding. "Another of your tests, Oramis. You took a great risk with our safety."

"I had every confidence that Baraapa wouldn't allow her to escape. You can let her go now."

Phoena felt the Viscount flinch. "I won't," he replied. She considered the dismissive way the other noblemen were treating him. They weren't his friends. A different emotion awoke. She knew what it was like to be a pawn in someone else's game. She smiled at the smaller nobleman.

Baraapa seemed to understand and dropped one of his arms. But the other remained loosely around her waist.

The remaining noblemen watched this silent negotiation. "I told you he had an advantage over us," Oramis said. "A pity he lacks the courage to steal a kiss."

Those words evoked a different reaction in each of them. The arm around Phoena's waist tightened. "I wish that bucket *had* contained water," Baraapa said. "She might have drowned you."

Her heart smashed against her ribs like a bird trying to escape a cage as someone grabbed her hand. Karilion's voice was beside her. "Oramis, you fool!"

Everything went dark.

She was falling again.

CHAPTER 9:
LOST IN THE RIVER

Water surrounded her, above and below. Phoena held her breath and rested. In the stillness, a memory from her childhood awakened. The event had happened in her first year in the *Academy* kitchens. She could have been no older than four, still oblivious to her peril. The older children from the kitchen were chasing her. This was not unusual. She was already an expert at hiding. Soon, they would grow tired of searching for her...

But that fateful day, she had been too slow. Her escape into the back garden had ended with her capture. Hate-filled words of prejudice spewed from her tormentors' lips, yet she maintained her silence.

There were no answers to their accusations. Experience had taught her that pleading for mercy only made things worse. The children dragged her towards the pond, which was shielded from the view of those in the kitchen. On the previous day, the cook had drowned a litter of unwanted kittens there.

Her child's mind accepted their reasoning.

Phoena hadn't struggled when they pushed her under the water. A strange hush fell on the group, while the bubbles of air gurgled from her mouth and nose. She had kept her eyes open, memorising their faces. When her vision blurred, the forbidden prayer had awoken within her. It sang with a loud voice, chasing away all thought except surrender.

The darkness had claimed her. But she hadn't drowned. It seemed but a heartbeat later, she was no longer a victim to those cruel hands. Instead, the warm sun was shining on her face. Phoena stood alone in a forbidden garden beside a river, her hair and clothes dripping wet.

She was almost dry by the time she found her way through the front gardens to the servants' entrance. Her return to the kitchen had been greeted by a severe scolding from the adults. The other children had never confessed their part in her drenching. They left her alone after that.

Phoena forced her mind from the memories as she drifted beneath the cold water. The current flowed faster here, drawing her along. She let some of the air in her lungs escape in a stream of bubbles. Those glistening spheres rose upward. She reached out her hand. A swirling brightness near her fingertips brought her comfort.

Thank you, Phoena silently prayed, I don't want to die alone in the darkness...

A shock ripped through her body. If she was alone, where were the three noblemen who had been in the dark cavern? They had said they needed her to guide them to freedom. Were they lost in the underground tunnels without hope of rescue?

Desperately, she recalled their images. Dark-haired Lord Karilion, so full of self-assurance. Viscount Baraapa, small and brown, stubborn and reckless. And the dragon, Lord Oramis.

I didn't mean to abandon them to the darkness, her mind cried. Please save them!

Above her, a blinding light banished the darkness. Using the last of her strength to push herself upwards, her head burst through the surface of the water. Phoena spluttered, gasping for air.

A shadowy form descended and fierce talons plucked her from the water. The black dragon delivered her to the bank and dropped her beside the underground river. Phoena rolled onto her side, coughing up water. She then lay still with her eyes closed.

"Baraapa, this is your fault," Karilion muttered. "You should be careful not to put ideas in her head. We almost drowned when she transported us into the river."

"I only wanted her to drown *him*."

"Be thankful that she didn't," Karilion said. "Without his ability to fly, we wouldn't have been able to rescue her. The current is too strong here, and she was too far from the bank."

"Is she dead?" Baraapa asked.

"Of course not."

"Why was she suspended under the water?"

"I don't know. Perhaps she doesn't know how to swim?"

Oramis joined the conversation. "Or perhaps she wanted to put as much distance between her and us as possible."

Phoena opened her eyes. The three noblemen crouched in a semi-circle three paces away from her. The familiar illuminating orb hovered above her head. That explained the brightness, but there was no accompanying warmth. She shivered. The three men were in a pitiful state. Puddles of water pooled beneath their sodden boots.

"I've gathered some driftwood," Lord Oramis said, "but I'm too cold to make flames. If we don't want to freeze to death, we'll have to persuade her to make fire."

"How do you propose we do that?" Lord Karilion asked. "I don't want to do anything to alarm her. When you suggested Baraapa kiss her, she looked as surprised as the rest of us when the portal opened."

Phoena pulled herself upright. "Don't talk about me as if I'm not here."

She rearranged her damp skirts as the three noblemen rose to their feet.

"You could try asking her," Baraapa said.

The others didn't respond. Baraapa took a deep breath and stepped closer. When he held out his hand, Phoena accepted it.

He bowed his head for a moment. "Your Ladyship," he began, "we, um, we... your humble and devoted servants, wish to apologise... to apologise for the shameful way we have behaved towards you. We deserved to be almost drowned—"

"Hey!" Karilion said, shoving him aside. "Don't overstep your authority." He snatched Phoena's hand from Baraapa.

"What he's trying to say is we want to declare a truce. We'll forget about the wager, and no longer make sport at your expense. In return, you'll answer our questions so we can find out how you activate your power."

"Enough talking," Oramis muttered. "I'm sorry, Your Ladyship, but I'm too cold for niceties." He pointed at the mountain of driftwood behind him. "Light the fire."

The glowing orb rose to illuminate the whole area. This was a different cavern. The ceiling was only half as high here. They were marooned on a ledge beside the underground river. Phoena could make out where the torrent came through a dark tunnel far away, while in the opposite direction, it raced away into the gloom.

While she puzzled over how to proceed, her mind whispered a prayer for guidance. She circled the driftwood, waiting for inspiration. The three noblemen walked a few steps behind her.

Phoena rubbed her hands to warm them. Her eyes kept wandering to the glowing light above her. She shivered again and then stopped. "Lord Karilion, is that an illumination spell that you have learned or does the power to make it work come from within you."

"It's my own power," he replied, and he waved his hand. The glowing orb danced in response.

"He's always boasting about how easy it is," Baraapa added.

"So if I have any power," Phoena said, "I should be able to work out how to do this?"

"It would be easier than making fire," Karilion said, "and Oramis seems certain that you can do that. Here, take my light and see what you can do with it."

The light source dropped onto Karilion's palm, and he held it towards her. Cautiously, Phoena touched it with her fingers. She prayed silently that something would happen.

The orb flashed brighter as she pressed her hand to the surface. She frowned and focused all her attention on willing something happen.

The glowing ball throbbed and vibrated under her hand.

It seemed to be getting warmer.

A few moments later, the orb exploded with a loud bang. Karilion swore as he pulled back his hand. All that remained of the orb was a glowing spiral of sparks, which fizzed and faded. The heavy darkness pressed in upon them.

A string of curses disrupted the ensuing silence. Karilion cried, "What did you do to my light?"

Phoena bit her lip.

"Make another one, Karilion," Baraapa said. "You're always boasting about how easy these *simple* tricks are. What's taking you so long?"

"I told you her defences push back," Karilion complained. "My ears are ringing. And I'm tingling all over. And my power won't work. It feels as if I've been struck by lightning."

Phoena turned in the direction of his voice and tried to find him in the darkness. "Give me your hand, Karilion."

"Why would I do that? You'll only blast me again."

"Just do as she says," groaned Oramis, "and stop complaining."

When Phoena felt a groping hand brush against her arm, she seized it. "I'll try again." She closed her eyes. She brought up the memory of the warmth she had felt moments before the orb exploded. The image turned within her mind.

She thought about the heat of the sun on her face on those rare occasions when she had walked in the garden. A thousand invisible needles pierced her fingers. Heat ran up and down her arm.

Karilion screamed and threw himself backwards, breaking her hold. The ground beneath her feet rumbled, and she fell to her knees.

"Whoo-hoo!" Baraapa shouted. "Now that's what I call a light! Hey, open your eyes. See what you've done!"

Phoena blinked in surprise. She shielded her face with one hand and stared at the ceiling. A miniature golden sun was spinning in place above them. Was she responsible for this marvel? The cavern was bright with warm light.

The damp misery in her soul began to shift.

"I'm still cold," Oramis muttered. "You've proven you have power, so light the fire."

"Give me your hand."

Karilion still knelt on the ground. "I'd be careful if I were you. She only sent a blast of energy through me, but she could burn you to a crisp."

"Thanks for the warning. I still have enough power to shape-shift." The air around Oramis wavered, and then his body began to shrink.

A few moments later, a tiny dragonet hovered before her. Phoena held out her hand. He settled on her wrist, coiling his tail around her arm. The dragonet turned his head towards the unlit bonfire.

Again, she closed her eyes. This time, she imagined the tiny orange flames that had revealed the dragon's presence in the garden. All she needed was a spark. She took a deep breath and concentrated.

"Please let this work, please let this work," she whispered.

The air seemed to crackle with energy, and her hand became painfully hot.

Whoosh! Phoena fell backwards to the ground. When she looked again, the driftwood was ablaze with an unnatural intensity. She watched the sparks exploding upward as the timber burned. The dragonet nuzzled her cheek, before lifting into the air. He dived into the crackling flames. He's safe now, she thought.

She shuddered as the realisation of what she had done hit her with full force. Turning from the fire, Phoena tried to process the revelation. At first, she was numb all over. Then a pain erupted in her chest. Perhaps her heart was being torn apart? Her body flashed hot, then cold, then hot again.

All her muscles tensed, and she was almost sick. Her head began to spin. The dizziness dropped her to the ground.

Baraapa bent down beside her. "Are you okay?"

"I need a few moments to recover. You go to the fire and dry yourself, My Lord."

His feet shuffled away. It was a relief to be alone.

Unfamiliar images flooded her mind as her thoughts turned inward. Were these forgotten memories?

The images flashed too fast for her to comprehend them. There were unfamiliar faces. Her emotional response was overwhelming. Some faces filled her with joy, while others inspired horror and despair. A vast treasury of emotions unlocked within her. She remained silent, not wanting to draw attention to herself.

The visions intensified until she lost her connection with the real world.

A younger version of Lord Westernbrooke appeared among these memories. He picked her up with his massive hands and placed her in an impossibly small box. The lid closed. She was alone in the darkness. Phoena screamed. But no sound reached her ears.

She tried to force her way out of the box. The harder she pushed, the more constrictive the barrier. There were flashes of light. Sparks flashed and whizzed in the confining space.

It seemed that she was in the box for an eternity. The mysterious sparks grew dimmer and dimmer until she had no power left...

A fierce pain stabbed her chest. Phoena fell forward. Her breathing came in ragged gasps. Baraapa shouted in alarm. He called for Karilion. Together they helped her to the fire.

"You'll feel better when your clothes are dry," Karilion said. The two men held her upright until she was certain she could stand by herself. They withdrew but stayed close.

The steam began to rise from her dress. From time to time she turned around, until her garments were completely dry. The bonfire died down to half its height.

A sudden flash of movement signalled the dragonet's awakening.

He rose from the glowing coals and spiralled around the artificial sun. He seemed to be increasing in size, with red streaks flashing along his black flanks. When the dragon towered over them, he flew towards the river.

The dragon returned, carrying more dripping driftwood.

He dropped this into the flames. There was a hiss followed by a sizzling explosion. This was no ordinary fire.

The two noblemen retreated. The dragon dipped his wings and flew away again.

Phoena stepped to the riverbank to watch the dragon's flight. Her two companions murmured behind her.

"What would happen if she tried to use her talent while holding your hand, Baraapa?" Karilion asked.

"As you so often *remind* me, I don't have any magic."

The dragon returned with more driftwood. Phoena watched him drop the timber onto the flames. She shielded her eyes from the sparks.

"I don't think that matters. I'm almost certain she only used Oramis and me to focus her mind."

"Ah," Baraapa said. "That's logical. She copied your magic light and replicated his dragon fire. What do you propose she might gain from me?"

"You're good with words. Let's see what she can do with that."

The dragon returned, delivered the final load and then dipped out of view on the other side of the fire.

Phoena refocused on the others.

"What would I talk about?" Baraapa asked.

"I remember your boast about your name-day celebration. I'm hungry. Let's see if she can conjure up a feast."

"Why do you think I can do that?" Phoena asked.

"You still doubt yourself. It can't hurt to see what else you can do."

"Can we wait until Oramis joins us? If something goes wrong, I don't want to lose anyone."

"If what goes wrong?" Oramis asked as he appeared beside Baraapa.

"Karilion wants her to try her magic on me, and 'conjure up a feast'."

"An excellent idea. A good bonfire always makes me hungry. I almost swept down and gobbled the three of you up, but then I remembered I need *her* to get me out of here."

"You promised not to tease her," Baraapa warned him.

"Karilion promised, not me. If you remember, I told her what I needed, and she did it. She doesn't want to lose any of us, so what is there for me to fear?"

"This," said Phoena, without thinking. With a flick of her wrist, she drew a wave from the river. Water splashed towards him. He jumped back. Her mouth opened in horror.

"Quick," shouted Baraapa. The three noblemen threw themselves at Phoena. They knocked her to the ground, creating an untidy stack of bodies.

They held their positions for longer than she believed necessary. When they finally released her, Phoena brushed the dirt from her skirt. She glowered at them but maintained her silence.

"Progress," Oramis said. His grin was contagious. "My Lady, words cannot express my gratitude that you didn't transport us somewhere else. You must be getting used to our disreputable company. Now, let's get on with this plan to create a feast."

"My lords, I have a few questions first. You threw yourselves at me because you feared I was going to leave without you?"

They all nodded. "Lord Karilion and Viscount Baraapa were holding me when I disappeared last time. Why weren't they beside me when I awoke in the river?"

"My Lady, if you must insist on formality," Karilion said with a bow, "I request your permission to answer that question."

"Don't call me 'my lady'. My name is Phoena." The words hung in the air.

She had never spoken her name out loud before.

"At last," Karilion laughed, "I have your name." For a moment, he looked as if he had forgotten the wager was off. Oramis punched his arm. Karilion rubbed the injured limb and then shrugged. "Phoena, that's a delightful name for a fire-adept enchantress. If I'm permitted to call you by your name, then you must drop the formalities. Address me as Karilion. I'm sure Baraapa won't mind what you call him. I'll leave our esteemed dragon-lord to speak for himself."

"Lady Phoena," Oramis said, bowing low. "My Lady, must I remind you that I was the first of our company to make your acquaintance. Indeed, I am heartbroken – nay, I am deeply offended – that you didn't notice my talons attached to your shoulder when you last *disappeared*." He bowed again. "To show that you repent of this oversight, please address me as Oramis."

Something fizzed inside Phoena. A spark of joy leapt into existence. She choked back a giggle and dropped into a curtsey.

"Are you mocking me?" Oramis asked, his eyes twinkling. "You forget that I'm a terrible tease." He moved closer.

Phoena danced out of his reach, giddy with unfamiliar happiness. She lifted her skirts and leapt over the smouldering fire. "You have to catch me first."

She led Oramis a merry chase. Phoena wasn't sure if he was letting her win, or whether there was something inexplicable about the way she eluded him. Finally, he paused beside the fire, out of breath.

CHAPTER 10:
TALKING THEIR WAY OUT

Karilion coughed. "If the two of you have finished your game, I have an answer to Phoena's question."

He reached for her hand. Karilion drew her closer to the smouldering fire. "There is no doubt that while we are in contact, you can transport us with you. But as soon as the portal opens to your destination, your defensive wards throw us away. They separate us to minimise our threat to you.

"Come, sit here, and lean against me," Karilion continued. She hesitated, glancing to the others.

He turned to the others. "Baraapa and Oramis, take your place on either side of Her Ladyship. I'm sure – now that she has accepted us as her companions – she will be able to sit beside us without fear. Perhaps now the wards won't see us as a threat."

Phoena sat, wrapping her arms around her bent knees with her feet flat on the ground. She gazed into the dying flames. Oramis rested his back against her knees. He was still very hot. Karilion reclined behind her. She could feel his breath on her neck as his hand played with her curls.

Baraapa stood staring into the darkness behind them. "How long do you think we've been in these caves?"

Karilion stirred. "That depends on whether time was involved in the transport. My stomach tells me I've missed luncheon, and it must be close to dinner now."

"Do you think Lord Westernbrooke is still waiting?"

"Where are you going with these questions?"

"If her talent works the way you expect," Baraapa said, "then what I describe will have an impact. Would it better for me to describe in detail the reception room where we met with Lord Westernbrooke?"

"What makes you think we'll go anywhere?" Phoena asked.

Baraapa dropped down beside Phoena and lifted one of her hands. "My Lady, you said you didn't want to try this experiment if our group wasn't complete. And Karilion has been careful in telling us where to sit. I suspect this is our best chance to get out of these caverns."

"We could go anywhere or nowhere," Karilion told him. "I want to test whether the words Phoena hears influence her power. That's why I suggested Baraapa talk about his name-day feast. If we arrive at your family home, Baraapa, then we'll have an answer. She's never been there. But if my guess is correct, she will take us out of this tomb, back to the Academy."

She sighed.

Oramis smiled towards her, and Baraapa squeezed her hand. Phoena looked at her feet. She didn't want them to know about her disappointment.

If they returned to the Academy, the closeness between them would be no more. But it wasn't fair to keep them underground for a moment longer.

Karilion leaned forward to speak in her ear. "I'm leaving it to you to make the right choice. I trust Baraapa's logic to guide you. One thing you should consider is whether you want answers. Lord Westernbrooke must have had something important to discuss with you."

"We should get started, then," Phoena said.

"Before I talk about my name-day feast," Baraapa said, "let me tell you a favourite tale from my childhood to warm up my voice. My old nurse said it was my mother's favourite story when she was a child. A long time ago, in a faraway land, there lived a prince."

"They're always the best kind of story," Oramis told Phoena. "But I always wonder what happens to all the ugly princes."

"Let him tell his story," Phoena said. "I'm hoping for a happy-ever-after ending."

"Thank you, Phoena," Baraapa said, smiling at her. "The handsome prince lived a lonely life in a faraway land. He was young and longed for adventures, but he knew his duty was to his people. His parents were the reigning king and queen. They were old, and he had no brothers and sisters. So he spent his days doing princely things. Growing weary while he waited for something interesting to happen.

"He had few friends. One by one, the few he had left him to go out into the world and seek their fortune. The news came back that each had found their perfect bride, and would never return. He dutifully sent them his best wishes and the obligatory gift."

"I always wonder what kind of gift a prince sends to a friend after they abandon him," Karilion said. "Would he resist the temptation to attach a transport spell that dragged his friend home?"

"With or without the bride?" Oramis asked.

"The gift doesn't matter," Baraapa said. "It's the prince's story that's important. There was an ancient prophecy that foretold the downfall of his kingdom. He must marry a true princess before he ascended to the throne. The years passed. The elderly king grew weaker and weaker. The people began to ask if the lonely prince would find a true princess before it was too late."

"Phoena wants a happy ending," Karilion reminded him. "Your prince seems destined for a dismal end."

"That's what everyone thought," Baraapa said. "At first, the people were content to whisper about the prince's situation. But soon they were discussing his lack of a bride in the marketplace. Questions were asked about his suitability as a monarch if he was so unlucky in love."

"Just because he couldn't find a true princess doesn't mean he was 'unlucky in love'." Karilion tugged Phoena's hair. "Everyone knows that princes are free to take liberties with all the maidens in the land."

She slapped his hand. "Not this prince. If the prophecy insists on a true princess, then he has to prove himself true, or she won't have him."

"Well said," laughed Oramis. "Karilion, she's heard of your reputation and given you notice to behave."

Baraapa waited until they resumed their silence. "The lonely prince decided to take action. He went to his parents and told them that he must go in search of the true princess. The queen asked him to delay his departure. She told him that if a true princess did not arrive within a year and a day, he would be free to journey in search of her."

He paused.

"Get on with the story," Oramis said.

"I was waiting for one of you to interrupt me again. You haven't, so I'll have to do it myself. What's with the phrase 'a year and a day'?" Baraapa asked. "That sets up the expectation that the true princess will only turn up at the end. Surely, a year is long enough to wait. Why add that extra day?"

"Oramis should answer that question," Karilion said. "Have you considered his sudden appearance at the Academy in our final year? Perhaps he had to leave home to seek a bride."

"That makes no sense," Oramis said. "If I was seeking a princess, why would I enrol in an all-male Academy."

Karilion and Baraapa nodded towards Phoena.

She shook her head in disbelief, her cheeks glowing. "Please continue the story, Baraapa. There are no princesses at the Academy. The lonely prince had better search elsewhere for his happiness."

Baraapa chuckled. "The days passed until only one day remained until the prince was freed from his promise. That morning, the sky was overcast. By midday, a terrible storm had descended on the land. There had never been a storm like it. A few hours later, a knock came at the castle door. The prince happened to be there to answer, and welcomed a caravan of wet strangers into the courtyard. The small party included a very bedraggled—"

"Bedraggled?" Karilion cried. "That's a strange word! I always envision the princess dressed in rags and ready for bed. Of course, the prince would be a proper gentleman and pretend he didn't notice her bed-readiness."

Baraapa coughed. "Soaked by the storm, the maiden was in a terrible state. Her uncle begged the prince to offer them hospitality. He told the prince that his niece was a princess on her way to a distant kingdom to consider an offer of marriage. The prince was immediately interested and ran off to tell his mother. 'A princess has come!' The queen urged him to be cautious. Not everyone who claims to be a princess—"

"Or not to be a princess," laughed Karilion.

"Ignore him," Phoena said.

Baraapa patted her hand. "I'm almost finished. The prince was impatient, but he knew better than to go against his mother's wishes."

"Wise man," muttered Karilion. "Have either of you met my mother? If she knew about half the mischief I get up to at the Academy, she'd curtail my freedom."

Phoena sighed.

Baraapa smiled. "The queen welcomed the travellers. She escorted the princess to a special bedchamber—"

"Aha!" cried Karilion. "The queen took one look at the bedraggled princess—"

Phoena shushed him. "If you interrupt one more time…"

Karilion mimed sewing his lips closed.

Baraapa spat out the next words at a faster pace. "The special bedchamber had a single bed, made up of layers of thick mattresses. The pile rose so high that the princess had to climb a ladder to get into bed. The queen left the princess alone.

"The next morning, the queen returned to ask the maiden how she had slept. The princess said the bed was terrible. There was something hard and lumpy under the mattress. The queen had the servants take away all the mattresses, and right on the bottom was a tiny pebble—"

"It was a pea!" exclaimed Karilion, and then covered his mouth. His eyes were laughing.

"On the bottom was a tiny pebble. Only a true princess would be able to feel such a tiny pebble under all those mattresses, the queen said. She told the prince to marry the princess."

"And they all lived happily ever after," declared Karilion. "Now you've finished your fairy tale, get on with talking about the food. I'm starving."

CHAPTER II:
ONLY
A
DREAM?

Phoena sat beside the fire as Baraapa talked about his name-day feast. She half-listened to his description of the delicious food that was served.

Each nobleman made enthusiastic comments about their favourite choices. He spoke well, but she lacked enthusiasm for the spirited debate.

Something had changed in her character during the previous story.

She felt strong and warm, inside and out.

Comfortable and comforted.

Safe.

As she turned over this new idea, her heart thumped in her chest. Were her fingers tingling? Should she interrupt her companions and warn them?

Phoena hesitated.

When had she ever been in a situation where anyone showed real interest in what she had to say?

Was she free to speak her mind with these young men?

Was this what it felt like to have true friends?

Was that the hidden meaning Baraapa had wanted her to discover in his fairytale?

Phoena smiled as she listened to them arguing.

There was no need to tell them about this pain in her chest that wouldn't desist.

She closed her eyes.

The next thing she knew, she was lying on a carpeted floor. When her eyes adjusted to the gloom, she recognised the darkened reception room. She was back in the *Westernbrooke Academy* guest apartment. The fire in the grate had gone out. The curtains were drawn.

She dragged herself upright and groaned, longing for the comforting light of the golden sun from the cavern. She threw a glance towards the candelabra. What a pity the candles were unlit.

Phoena sighed. Her imagination must be playing tricks on her. Did a tiny flame flash in midair? She checked again, and her heart leapt. One by one, the candles burst into flame.

She must have fallen asleep in the cavern and entered a dream.

The tea-things were still arranged on the table. One delicate cup lay smashed on the floor where she had dropped it hours before. She walked around the table and picked up the fragile pieces.

With her head bowed in prayer, the maid turned the pieces over in her hand. Her fingers tingled, and something shifted in her hand. She stared at the perfect cup. There was no indication that the delicate object had ever been broken.

Phoena smiled. Definitely a dream.

She collected the matching saucer and put them both on the tray. Next, she selected a piece of shortbread. This was something she would never do in real life.

Her stomach grumbled, and she nibbled the sweet treat. It was even more delicious than she imagined.

Careful not to indulge her greed, she left the remaining shortbread on the plate. This was a servant's dream.

Phoena hummed to herself as she gathered the trays and ferried them to the counter. Next, she went to the fireplace, where she laid a fresh fire. She kept her eyes open and imagined a tiny puff of flame. There was a satisfying whoosh, as the fire burst into life.

She hugged herself, whirling around in joyful dance before she set the kettle to boil. While Phoena waited, she emptied the teapot and organised the equipment needed to wash the tea set. When the kettle boiled, she filled the small basin and set to work.

"She seems very happy," a voice said from behind her. She didn't turn. None of this was real, so it didn't matter if she ignored Oramis.

"You would think she'd be wondering where we disappeared to," Karilion said. "Yet see how she sings and dances without us."

"You're not real," she laughed. "This is my dream, and I'm not letting two spoilt noblemen ruin it."

"Who are you calling *spoilt*," Karilion cried. Phoena whirled to face him, splashing water in his direction. He ducked. Oramis became the unintended victim.

Water dripped down Oramis' face, and he wiped his hands on his waistcoat. "My Lady, you owe me an apology."

Phoena lifted her skirts and dashed further away. The two young men looked at each other and grinned. Both of them began chasing her around the room. With unexpected energy, Phoena leapt over furniture. Her laughter filled the room.

"Very un-Ladylike behaviour," Oramis said.

"But much more to my liking," Karilion replied. "If I didn't know our enchantress so well, I'd think she was flirting with us."

"I most certainly hope not," a big voice declared. "Lady Firebird, what is the meaning of this outrageous behaviour."

Phoena came to an abrupt halt. There in the doorway stood Lord Westernbrooke, with Matron at his side. Baraapa was peering around them at the scene.

"What are you doing in my dream?"

"She still thinks this is a dream," Karilion said to Oramis as they crept closer. "If I didn't know Lord Westernbrooke could exile me, I'd take advantage of her mistake and steal a kiss."

"Don't," Phoena said, and with a flick of her wrist, she transported Karilion out into the hallway. This achievement was easy in her dream.

Her life at the *Academy* would be different if she had real power. She could hear his loud protest through the open door. She spun towards his companion.

"And you, Oramis?" She wiggled her fingers at him. "Where would you like me to send you? There's a delightful pond in the back garden."

She enjoyed the stricken look on his face.

"Forgive me, Phoen–, umm, Lady Firebird." Oramis bowed low as he backed away. "But if you could send me and my fellow adventurers to Karilion's apartment, we would be grateful."

"I grant your request." With a wave of her hand, he vanished.

She looked towards the doorway. Lord Westernbrooke and Matron were staring at her. She bobbed briefly and turned her back on them. With a song, she returned to her washing up.

When she finished, she put the tea set away and turned to face the room. The two adults were now seated on separate sofas. "Oh, you're still here. Perhaps I should offer you a cup of tea?"

"That won't be necessary," Matron said, rising from the sofa. She tilted Phoena's head back and examined her eyes. "You're overexcited and feverish. But that's not unexpected, considering the adventure you've had."

"Taking off on her own with three young men," Lord Westernbrooke growled. "That is not the kind of *adventure* my goddaughter should have."

"What kind of adventure should I have?" Phoena put her hands on her hips. "Are you going to put me back in the box and leave the darkness to rob me of my joy?"

Lord Westernbrooke frowned. The girl shook her finger at him. "You call yourself my godfather, but I've suffered terribly under your care."

She paused to breathe. "For fourteen years, I've known nothing but loneliness and isolation. As an orphan in a house filled with magic users, I've been the victim for all the worst kind of tricks. And then I discover that it's all a lie. I do have some kind of power, but I'm surrounded by controlling protections to stop me from using it."

She opened her hand.

A stream of sparks filled the air.

"Then, I find myself cast out into the darkness without any way of helping myself. I was lost. If it hadn't been for those three young men, I would never have found my way home."

She lifted her eyes, and a tiny golden sun rose in front of her. For a moment, she forgot everything except the wonder of her creation.

She bowed towards Lord Westernbrooke. "Forgive me for my impertinence, sir. But after the dangers I've faced today, a little silliness in my own dream should be permissible."

The giant rose to his full height and shouted at her. "This. Is. Not. A. Dream."

"Oh! I don't like this dream anymore."

Matron leapt forward, but she was too late.

CHAPTER 12:
FINALLY
ALONE

Lonely silence pressed upon Phoena's ears. The darkness was thick and confining – definitely real. She fought tears. From now on, she would speak her thoughts and prayers aloud. "Where am I now?"

There were no companions to answer her. At least those three young men were warm and safe. If they were fortunate, they would be enjoying dinner with their real friends in the dining hall.

"What does it matter if I'm here, and they are there?" she chided herself. "The madness would not have lasted. They had to go back to their noble lives, and I– and I– Oh, foolish, foolish girl! You sit in the darkness, weeping for a future that can never be. You only have yourself to blame."

Phoena forced herself to stand.

"Please, can I have some light?" She didn't know who she asked. Nor did she expect a reply.

There came a blinding flash, and suddenly her golden sun was shining overhead.

"Fire?" she asked the darkness.

A pile of glowing coals appeared on the ground at her feet.

"I'm going to need some fuel for the fire."

Before she could move, strange objects started dropping from the ceiling. She ran over and picked up one of the massive twisted things. It looked like the root of a plant, but it had the thickness and texture of a dried branch. She dragged it across to the fire. Immediately after she tossed it onto the coals, it caught alight. The flames were brighter and higher than she expected.

"Thank you," she cried, rushing about to collect her supply.

Sitting beside the fire, Phoena enjoyed the warmth. "All I need now is something to eat. I wonder what kind of soup the young men are—"

Before she completed the sentence, a bowl of steaming soup appeared beside her. The engraved handle on the fine silver spoon was familiar. As she reached for the bowl, a crusty bread roll landed in her lap. Phoena ate her soup, taking her time to savour each mouthful. It was a generous serve. The soup was thick, full of chunky meat and vegetables. She used the bread to wipe the bowl clean.

When Phoena had eaten every mouthful, she investigated her surroundings. This cave had no exit. She paced the width and depth. It was a much smaller space than before, made even cosier by the central fire. If those noblemen were here, it would be a tight space. She pondered the rising smoke. It disappeared through the ceiling without robbing the cavern of oxygen.

Was the cave smaller because she was alone?

"I need answers."

Immediately, the atmosphere changed.

Phoena scanned the cavern. On the opposite wall, a glowing spiral of light drew her attention. As she approached, the spiral resolved itself into a mirror with a gilded frame. It positioned itself on the wall at the right height for her to view her reflection.

"That's not what I expected."

The face that looked out at her was unfamiliar. There was enough likeness that she knew it was her face. But all the imperfections that she had lamented were transformed. She raised her hand to the end curls that framed her face. The hand in the mirror did the same. Was this what she looked like, or was this an illusion?

Phoena closed her eyes for a moment. She tried to remember the features of the three noblemen who had been drawn into her adventure. When she opened her eyes, the image in the mirror had shifted.

Now she could see the dining hall as if she were standing in the servants' doorway. As she focused her attention, the image grew clearer. It was almost as if she walked across the room. Karilion, Baraapa and Oramis sat together. They leaned close to each other. Phoena listened to their conversation.

"It doesn't mean anything," Karilion said. He had the central seat. "Just because your bowl of soup disappeared before you could eat it, Oramis. And just because your bread disappeared at the same time, Baraapa. That doesn't mean she likes either of you more than me. In fact, it means the opposite. She knew I was hungry."

"I'm not worried about the soup," Oramis said. "I want to know how she managed to remove both items without any warning."

"Do you think she put a tracer on us?" Baraapa asked, his eyes alert as he looked around the room. "I can't see her here."

"She could be here, and none of us would notice," Karilion said. "Our mysterious lady has gained more control over her talent."

"Do either of you know who she is?" Baraapa asked. "She seemed surprised to discover she had any talent, and she was very convincing as a servant."

"Lord Westernbrooke called her Lady Firebird," Oramis said. "I'm not familiar with that title."

"You should ask the man himself," Karilion said. "He's walked into the room, with Matron at his side. I don't like the way he's glaring at us. I'd transport myself out of here, but Lord Westernbrooke has put the dining hall in lockdown."

Phoena watched as the image in the mirror twisted. Lord Westernbrooke's massive figure filled the frame. The dining hall fell silent as the students stared at the intimidating new arrival. Headmaster Pepperbry rose to his feet.

"Pepperbry," Lord Westernbrooke began, "I need to interview those students again."

Headmaster Pepperbry opened and closed his mouth like a fish out of water. "Lord Westernbrooke, can this not wait until after dinner?"

"It cannot!"

Matron rested her hand on Lord Westernbrooke's arm. "Cousin, don't make a scene." She smiled at Headmaster Pepperbry. "Thank you, Headmaster. With your permission, I will deliver Lord Westernbrooke's invitation."

The tall woman approached the young men's table.

Oramis rose to his feet and bowed. Baraapa copied him. Karilion lifted one eyebrow, looked down at his plate, and sighed. "If I must," he said. He remained seated, but he swivelled towards her. "Matron, you wish to speak with us?"

Matron's eyes narrowed as she waved her hand. Phoena watched threads of glowing light flash across the gap between them. "Please excuse the intrusion, Lord Karilion, Viscount Baraapa and Lord Oramis."

A star-shaped sign appeared on each of the noblemen's foreheads as Matron spoke their names. "It has become necessary to ask you to return to the guest apartment at your earliest convenience. Lord Westernbrooke will receive you immediately after dinner. I have taken the liberty of marking you with the invitation, as a precaution."

She spun on her heels, ushering Lord Westernbrooke out of the dining hall.

"What kind of precaution?" Baraapa asked.

Oramis grinned. "They don't want us to escape."

"The barriers are still in place," Karilion muttered, rubbing his forehead. He looked at his fingers and frowned. "There's no way out of the dining hall."

Oramis laughed. "It's not 'out' they're worried about. They want to track us if she takes us further in."

"That means they've lost her again!" Karilion said. "I thought they knew how to prevent her escape."

"They're as clueless as we are about Her Ladyship's capabilities," Oramis said. The next course had been served. He reached for his fork and began to eat. "At least she's not interested in the rest of my dinner."

"Be careful what you say," Baraapa said, looking over his shoulder. He was staring straight at Phoena, but there was no sign of recognition in his eyes. "I don't have any magic," he said, "but I keep expecting to see her beside me."

She gasped and pulled back. Then she laughed at herself.

"You've got it bad," Karilion said.

"She wouldn't look twice at a non-magic like me."

"I don't think magical status means anything to her," Oramis said. "We're all outclassed." He paused with his fork halfway to his mouth. "I've been meaning to ask why you chose that particular fairytale."

Karilion laughed. "Oramis, it's clear that you're the prince in the story. You're in search of the princess."

"Nonsense," Oramis replied. "I'm not honourable enough to be the prince. I'm only here for this semester. If I don't succeed in infiltrating your society, then I'll be off to some far-flung colony to perfect my craft."

"I knew it!" Baraapa hissed. "You're a spy."

"Of course, but don't make it too well known. Nobody will tell me anything if they realise I'm untrustworthy."

"Nobody trusts you anyway," Karilion said. "You set yourself up to fail. There's some ulterior motive at play here, or you wouldn't have been so obnoxious."

"I'd pretend to take offence, but then I'd have to challenge you to a duel. I'm sure the Armoury Master's taking wagers on which of us will make the first move."

"Can't you two have a simple conversation without making it a contest."

"I'm offended, Baraapa," Karilion said, "that you think any of my exploits are 'simple'. You haven't answered Oramis' question. Why did you tell that story?"

"It was only a story. If you want to imagine some deeper motivation, that's up to you."

"I don't believe him for a minute," Karilion said to Oramis. "Nothing Baraapa says or does is without reason."

"I don't care what you think," Baraapa said. "She liked the story, and that's all that matters."

"What matters is she brought us back to the Academy," Oramis said, "and then banished us from her presence."

His brow furrowed, and he leaned over his plate. The others turned to their meals, and the conversation ended.

Phoena relaxed. She recalled the story and considered whether there was any hidden meaning. If she represented the princess in the story, what was Baraapa trying to tell her?

Rubbing her hands together, she walked back to warm herself by the fire. She sat on the ground, staring into the flames. Her mind drifted.

CHAPTER 13:
THE RIVER AWAKENS

It was colder when Phoena awoke. She frowned at the fire. All that remained was a small pile of charcoal nestled among the ashes. She shook herself and rubbed life into her numb legs.

The small artificial sun still hovered near the ceiling. In response to her glance, it intensified its radiant heat. She smiled, and the air grew warmer. She strolled around her cave. What should she do next?

She didn't know how long she had slept and was reluctant to return to the mystical mirror. She paused. Was she afraid that the vision would only reveal an empty dining hall? Or did she fear the mirror would show her one of the young men in the privacy of his bedchamber? Was there one lord over the others that she might hope to see?

Chiding herself for entertaining thoughts above her station, she resumed her pacing.

But what was her station? If Lord Westernbrooke was her godfather, why had he not contacted her before? Did his appearance mean she wasn't an orphan? Did he know what had happened to her parents? And did she have any other relatives?

There were too many questions, and no-one to advise her. "I have to go back."

Phoena pictured herself standing in the reception room in the guest apartment. Nothing happened. Did she need to concentrate on the faces of the people she wanted to meet? Lord Westernbrooke was difficult to visualise, so she thought about Matron instead.

The traumatised girl recalled that woman's kindness when she had discovered Phoena asleep outside her office. The memory was powerful, but it didn't change the maid's current situation.

"What am I doing wrong?"

Running to the mirror on the wall, Phoena placed her

hands upon the frame. "Show me what to do." She peered at the reflective surface, but all she could see was her face, with the cavern behind her.

Was that the wrong question?

She tried phrase after phrase until her throat was sore.

"I'm thirsty."

The ground shook, and she fell to her knees. When she recovered, she could hear a rushing sound, like water pouring into a kettle. Behind her, a stream of dark blue liquid poured from the wall at waist height.

Phoena rushed over and dipped her hand into the flow. Her fingers tingled, but not because the water was cold. This was not ordinary water. She hesitated for a moment, but nothing further happened. She scooped the strange water into her mouth.

It tasted sweet, like honey, but after she had swallowed it, her throat burned as if it was on fire. The burning sensation lasted only a few minutes.

Phoena drank some more.

She lost her fear of the heat that awakened inside her, gulping the blue water until her thirst was quenched. She hugged herself with delight. A spontaneous song of praise rose from within her. She sang and danced with all her strength. This new freedom dispatched all her worries.

Until she stepped into ankle-deep water.

Then she returned to the fountain pouring from the wall. Where the small trickle had begun, there was now a gushing waterfall. The hole in the wall continued to widen as more and more water poured into her cave. Within minutes, the whole cavern floor was awash.

"What am I supposed to do?"

Could she block the hole? She tore off her apron and pushed the bundled fabric into the opening. At first, this stemmed the flow but then cracks appeared in the surrounding wall. A gaping hole opened in the cavern wall through which more water flowed.

A foaming wave of blue water knocked Phoena off her feet. Carried along by the incoming breakers, she was unable to regain her balance. She smashed into the opposite wall, and everything went dim.

The next thing she knew, her lungs were on fire as she drifted beneath the water. Her chest still moved in and out with each breath, but it was water, not life-giving air that filled her lungs. Afraid that she was drowning, Phoena held her breath and pushed up towards the surface. Her long skirts wrapped around her legs. The waterlogged fabric made it impossible to rise.

The struggle to remove the heavy overdress sent her spiralling down. The descent continued until her feet touched the submerged cavern floor.

Frantically, she pulled the garment over her head, and it was torn from her hands by the current. Free of the cumbersome weight, she expected to rise, yet her feet remained firmly planted on the ground. Phoena looked up to where her golden globe shone through the waves. It still spun close to the ceiling. The surface of the water seemed so far away. Here on the bottom, the shadows grew darker and gloomier.

Bending her knees, she dropped into a crouch and jumped as high as she could. Her efforts brought no more reward than if she were attempting to fly. When she dropped back to the floor, Phoena repeated the process again and again. Exhausted, she sat down, wrapping her arms around her knees. She discovered it was impossible to weep and hold her breath at the same time.

A cry of woe escaped her. She swallowed a great mouthful of water, but something unexpected happened. Instead of suffocating, it was like taking a deep breath. She was breathing water as if it was life-giving air!

Her whole body trembled. How could this be? The fire within her chest was back, but she felt lighter. She leapt to her feet. The sudden movement lifted her from the floor. After experimenting with different movements, Phoena learned to direct her progress. She put her hands above her head as if she were reaching for the ceiling. Next, she pushed with her legs. With unexpected speed, she flew upwards.

When her head broke the surface, Phoena was giddy with delight. Her golden light source hovered high above the swirling water. She continued to rise until she was close enough to the ceiling to touch the rocky surface with her outstretched fingers. A moment later, she began to drop back towards the waves, where she bobbed on the surface. She wasn't conscious of summoning the sun, but the warm sphere flew to her.

The orb spun around her head, before plummeting under the waves. Phoena cried out. But instead of extinguishing, the marvellous light became transfused with silver. It changed from a glowing sun into a glistening moon. Now the waves around her shimmered with crystal brilliance. She ducked her head under the water. She could see a great distance in every direction. The silvery globe dropped deeper as she followed it down.

The massive opening where the water entered was impossible to ignore. As she pushed herself towards it, she was only half-aware that the silvery globe did not follow her.

Phoena made little progress against the surging torrent. When she ceased her effort, the current took her back towards the globe. She turned from the water's source, and the globe moved with her. There on the further wall was a shiny oval shape. She drifted towards it. It must be the mystical mirror.

Were shapes moving on the shimmering surface?

When she arrived, the mirror's reflective surface swirled with mist. Her hands gripped the decorative frame to hold her in place beneath the waves. At first, she saw nothing more. When the silvery moon floated nearer, a face appeared. Phoena leaned closer. Was this her reflection? She pulled faces at the mirror, and the maiden in the mirror responded with perfect synchronicity.

So much had changed since she last looked at herself in the mirror. She shook her head. Her hair floated around her head in long, glistening tendrils. Not only had it grown, but the colour had changed from a mousy-brown to a richer black-brown, like dark, tempered chocolate.

The colour reminded her of the soil in the vegetable garden, after heavy rain. Her dishwater-grey eyes were now the colour of the water that surrounded her – indigo blue with shimmering silver highlights. But the most dramatic change was her upturned mouth. There was a joy in her expression that she had never seen before. She pressed her hand towards the mirror in wonder. She was beautiful.

As soon as Phoena's hand touched the mirrored surface, there was a terrible shudder. She bounced back. The image in the mirror did the same. A massive crack divided the cavern wall from top to bottom. The rock wall crumbled before her. Jagged chunks of rock toppled inward. She put up her hands to defend herself. The sudden movement thrust her backwards through the water. She narrowly escaped being crushed by the rock slide.

An opening appeared where the wall had been. The water surged forward. For a moment, the mirror floated before her. Before she could catch it, the escaping water carried the mystical object into the unknown.

Phoena dove after it.

On the other side of the shattered wall, a violent churning replaced the silence of her cavern. She tumbled head over heels, and her thin petticoat drifted up over her head. She screamed as her hands wrestled with the fabric. As if in response, a thunderous roar erupted all around her. She could feel the powerful vibrations inside and out.

A moment later, she was falling. Her silvery moon tumbled with her, suspended near her head. Her new surroundings were terrifying. And breathtakingly beautiful.

Her stream plummeted through the darkness to join a majestic underground river. When she hit the surface of the indigo waters, she plunged into the cold depths. A school of silvery fish flashed away in every direction. They swam and danced beneath the waves. Phoena longed to follow them, but the water carried her onward at a furious pace. Her only choice was to surrender to it.

When she became accustomed to the speed, she noted her surroundings. The comforting silver moon floated nearby, bathing everything with a cool light. Wherever she looked, there was something marvellous to see. Rounded boulders covered the river bottom. Some were massive like a mansion, while others were small enough that she fancied she might be able to carry them in her arms. There was no time to try – the water moved her relentlessly onward.

Plants waved their elongated leaves in the current. Phoena tried to catalogue the profusion of living things that peeped out to stare at her silvery moon. The river teemed with a myriad of creatures. Many of these were unfamiliar, but she recognised some from her time as a scullery maid. Food was abundant here...

She abandoned herself to the journey. After a time, the water lost some of its forcefulness. The current slowed to a more comfortable pace and her silvery moon lessened in intensity. The water was no longer a uniform hue as coloured streaks disrupted the cold darkness.

Phoena propelled herself towards one of the lighter streaks, where the water seemed calmer. It was warmer here, and the lazy fish were larger.

They seemed more curious than afraid. One of them nibbled at her hair. She laughed and raised her hand. The fish flitted away but loitered nearby.

Something caught her attention. Was that the mystical mirror again? Phoena moved towards it. The mirror drifted into her hand, and she clutched it to her chest with both arms. Her eager movement sent her into a spin which propelled her back out into the stronger current. Before she could right herself, she was racing along.

Floating with her face towards the bottom, she watched the smooth rocks whizz past. On several occasions, she cried out as she crashed against an obstruction. The water was merciless, lifting her around the boulders and propelling her onward.

Then everything disappeared in a blinding flash of pain.

CHAPTER 14:
DRIFTING

When Phoena opened her eyes, her whole body ached. She drifted, with her arms outstretched. Those lifeless limbs were unresponsive. She still gazed upon the river bottom, with her floating petticoat bunched around her knees. For a moment, she forgot she could breathe underwater, and imagined she had drowned.

Her galloping heart insisted she was still alive, yet it was a long time before she was calm again.

Wherever she was, it was harder to make out the details of her surroundings. The silvery globe had left her. The current was slow, the murky water tainted a muddy brown. She peered through the gloom.

Grey flashes came and went, sleepy fish swimming this way and that. One bumped into her. With a gentle flip of its tail, it swam around her and continued on its way. Phoena could not follow it.

A dark shape lifted from the mud beneath her. A momentary glimmer convinced her that this was her mystical mirror. She longed to hold it again. The mirror floated along beneath her. After a time, she imagined she could hear voices. She was unable to draw the mirror close enough to see what was happening. So she concentrated on listening.

"Baraapa, I'm bored." That sounded like Karilion. "Going fishing is the worst suggestion you've had."

Phoena smiled as she drifted. The mirror was still tuned to the noblemen.

"You're complaining because you're no good at it, Karilion."

Karilion snorted. "You've only caught a single fish, and you had to let it go again because it was too small. If you weren't so stubborn, I could transport us to the market and buy enough fish to satisfy your pride."

"It's not about the fish," Oramis interjected. Good, the three of them were still together. "It's about 'enjoying the fresh air and the sunshine'."

"Oramis, don't lecture me," Karilion said. "You haven't even got your hook wet."

"There's plenty of time. I'm content to sit here, and listen to the two of you arguing."

"Ha!" Karilion replied. "You're so far from the water I'm beginning to think you're afraid."

"I'm no more afraid than you are," Oramis said. A big splash followed his words.

Clouds of mud swirled around her. What?

Phoena tried to locate the site of the disturbance, but she was still unable to move. The clay particles clung to her face and went up her nose. Ugh! Phoena coughed.

"Hey!" Baraapa yelled. "Stop that. You'll scare away the fish."

"Don't blame me," Karilion said. "Oramis is the one who jumped in the water. We have a good excuse now to pack up the fishing gear and go somewhere else."

"We came fishing," Oramis said, to an accompanying series of splashes. "Because we wanted to be away from the others without attracting too much attention."

"Which reminds me, Baraapa," said Karilion, "Where have those annoying twins gone? For as long as I've known you, they've shadowed your every move. What did you do to make them drop you? They've even swapped to a different dining table."

"When we disappeared with Phoena, they were left behind with three angry guardians. Lord Westernbrooke suggested they rethink their allegiance to me. He promised there would be 'dire consequences' when we returned."

"It's been three days," Karilion said. "I haven't seen any 'dire consequences'. But they must have passed on those warnings to the other fourth-years. Oramis and I are also shunned. This exclusion has ruined my social life. Why else would I spend this half-day holiday with two outsiders like you? It might be bearable if either of you had anything interesting to say. Why am I the one who always has to direct the conversation?"

"Hmmph!" Baraapa muttered. "There'd be plenty to talk about if either of you would answer my questions."

A loud plop was the only response to Baraapa's complaint. More of the same sound followed in rapid succession. As puffs of mud rose around her, Phoena realised some kind of projectile was being pelted into the river.

"Karilion!" Baraapa shouted. "Stop throwing rocks into the water!"

"He's bored," Oramis said. "Try asking Karilion your most pressing questions now."

The barrage continued. The water surrounding Phoena grew murkier by the minute. It became more difficult to breathe. Her mouth and nose were coated with particles of clay. In desperation, she tried to spit it out.

"You're only trying to distract me," Baraapa said, "but this time, it's not going to work. I'll keep asking questions until you give me some acceptable answers. First, I want to know what happened to her?"

"What makes you think I know anything you haven't already ascertained for yourself?" Karilion said.

"You've been trying to find her with your magic."

"So has Oramis. Why aren't you troubling him with your questions?"

"He's even less likely to give me a straight answer than you."

The only response was another barrage of rocks into the river.

Phoena cried out with her mind for him to stop. The assault ceased without any further comment from above.

Phoena was thankful, despite being uncertain whether she had influenced Karilion's actions.

The conversation resumed after a few minutes.

"I'm more concerned," Oramis said, "that Lord Westernbrooke has used *his* power, and been unable to find her."

"How do you *know* he hasn't found her?" Baraapa asked.

"We all saw him in the dining hall at breakfast. If she had been found, he'd be gone."

"What makes you so certain?"

Oramis laughed harshly. "It's obvious. He's already decided that we are unsuitable companions for his goddaughter. But she's formed an emotional attachment to us. As soon as he finds her, he'll magic her away from our wicked influence."

"He could have her locked in the guest wing."

"I don't think his power is strong enough to contain her," Karilion said.

"You're only guessing," Baraapa said. "It could be part of a plan to throw us off the trail."

"If that was true, you wouldn't have that magic tracker stuck in the middle of your forehead."

"I only have your word that there *is* a tracker."

"Both Oramis and I can see it. And we've told you that we each have one too. Matron's magic is sticky and impossible to remove."

There followed another long silence. A different sound disrupted the water immediately above her. After a few moments, a baited metal hook appeared within her limited view. She watched in horror as the sharp barbs floated towards her. When the hook drew near enough, it snagged the skin on her arm. She gasped. Tiny droplets of blood floated free to drift away on the current.

"There's something heavy on my line!" Baraapa said.

The hook tugged against her skin. A few moments later, the jagged metal pulled free. The sharp pain in her arm was matched by a pain in her heart. But then her hope was reborn. The current swirled and the hook snagged on her clothes.

The tugging intensified, and her petticoat responded. For a moment, she rose in the direction of the surface. Her joy awakened, only to die again. Her body was too heavy, and the fabric too weak – the hook tore free.

"I've lost it. I'll reel the line in and see if I've still got the bait."

There was a whispering sound above her.

"What's that on your hook?" Karilion asked.

"It looks like a piece of fabric," Baraapa replied. "There must be something down there."

"Send Oramis in to look. He's already wet."

"Anything to keep you two quiet," Oramis said. "If it's treasure, I'm not sharing."

There was another large splash. The clouds of mud stirred again. He must be coming closer, but she couldn't see him.

"If it's treasure," Karilion laughed, "you have to share. We've agreed to work together, and this fishing trip is part of the deal."

"A bit further out," Baraapa called. "Careful, visibility is poor there."

Phoena's anticipation rose. The pressure in her head intensified as the splashing disrupted the current.

A dark shadow blocked out the dim light from above. Her heart leapt when she felt something bump against her. Oramis had arrived. He lifted her hand towards the surface.

I'm here! her mind cried.

Almost immediately, his grip released her floating arm. A string of unfamiliar words burst from Oramis. She heard him in stereo, both from the mirror below and through the water above.

His shadow retreated.

No! Don't leave me here!

"What?" Karilion asked.

"You've found something?" Baraapa said at the same time.

"I've found a body," Oramis said.

"Then pull it out," Baraapa shouted. "We have to see who it is!"

"He already knows," cried Karilion, and she heard a second splash. He must be wading towards her. "Oramis! Don't leave her there. We have to get her out of the water."

"I've been praying that we would find her," Oramis said.

"But not like this."

"Oramis! Snap out of it!" Karilion said, seizing Phoena's body by the arms. "If you don't move, I'm going to hit you! We can't leave her under the water. Take her legs."

The pair heaved Phoena from the water. They dragged her up the riverbank where they dropped her onto the green grass.

"Roll her over," Baraapa shouted. "What is wrong with the two of you?"

Her body flopped over to face the cloudless sky. Baraapa came closer, peering at her face. Phoena blinked, and he shot backwards. "What kind of magic is this?"

She stared at the three noblemen who leaned over her. She couldn't breathe, and her chest threatened to explode.

Baraapa struggled out of his ruffled jacket and draped it across her body. "She's still alive. Quick, Karilion. Use your magic to take her back to the *Academy*. She needs a healing spell."

"I don't trust myself. What if she overwhelms my magic and we go somewhere—"

"Oramis—"

"No!"

Baraapa screamed in frustration. "You can't leave her to die. You have to do something!" He pulled out a handkerchief and rubbed at her face. "She's turning blue."

"Why is she opening and closing her mouth like that fish you landed?" Karilion asked.

Oramis swore. "Quick! Her mouth and nose are full of mud. She's suffocating."

Hands rolled her onto her side. Someone was hitting her between the shoulder blades. Hard, repetitive shocks that hurt.

Meanwhile, Baraapa stuck his fingers in her mouth. He scooped out some of the mud. Phoena gagged. Water and mud spewed forth all over him. Her body experienced a series of savage spasms, as she continued to cough and splutter. Finally, she took a deep breath. The shuddering stopped.

All three noblemen were leaning over her, keeping her on her side.

"Once again, it's Baraapa who found the solution," Oramis said.

"My Lady, we are so pleased to have you back with us," Karilion added. "But if you continue to frighten me like that, my hair will be grey before my time."

Baraapa sat back and frowned at her. "When did you find out you were a water-sprite?"

"A water-sprite?" Karilion shook his head at Baraapa. "You're showing your ignorance again. That's not—"

"You can't deny the evidence," Baraapa said, "She has power over water as well as fire. Is there any reason she can't be a water-sprite *and* a fire-affinity enchantress?"

Karilion looked off into the distance, and the other two noblemen waited for his reply. Phoena struggled to a seated position and glanced from face to face. She didn't know what a water-sprite was, but that phrase didn't feel right. And what about the other claim? There was no denying that she had an attraction to fire, but she doubted she was an enchantress. She had learned no spells, and knew no magical phrases. Perhaps it was a gift? That would explain the strange sensation that stirred deep inside her whenever she was near a fire. But what about the suggestion that she was a water-sprite? She swallowed, preparing to confess her ignorance.

Oramis shushed her. "Don't say anything. Let's hear what our expert has to say first."

Karilion shot Oramis a scornful look, before addressing Baraapa. "It wasn't *her* talents that I was disputing, but *your* failure to grasp the significance of the term you used. Don't you know that 'water-sprite' is a derogatory term. Don't judge this powerful domain on the performance of those silly girls you've seen at parties. They dabble with water-magic and their power is only an illusion. Take away their pretty costumes and silence their simple spells, and their fraudulent claims are easily dismissed. But there is nothing frivolous about what we have seen here. If I had to define her power, I'd say this fair maiden was a water-worker."

"I don't think you've grasped the significance of Baraapa's question," Oramis said. "While I agree that 'water-sprite' is too dismissive a term – I'd have used something else – he's asking whether she can be talented across two elemental domains."

"It's rare," Karilion said, "but not impossible for someone to be proficient in more than one domain. She's demonstrated talent with water and fire–"

"So you both agree she's a water-*worker*," Baraapa said. "*And* a fire-enchantress."

"You misunderstood me," Oramis said. "Not water *and* fire. I believe she is more powerful and mysterious than that. Now, don't interrupt me! I need to speak my mind before I lose courage. This Noble Lady is an elemental virtuoso!"

"B-but that m-means–" Baraapa's face drained of colour.

Oramis nodded. "That means she has powers across all the elemental domains. See how the mud still clings to her face. Remember, whenever she took fright, she transported us deep within the earth. She can breathe underwater and bend it to her will, and we've all seen her make fire."

"And the golden sun she conjured up draws energy from the air," Karilion added.

"No wonder Lord Westernbrooke wanted her hidden away from the world," Baraapa said.

He took another step backward. Then he dropped down onto one knee and bowed his head to the ground in front of her. "Lady, I offer you my allegiance and ask that you accept me as you're humble servant."

Oramis and Karilion stared at him before they both dropped down to join him.

CHAPTER 15:
THREE CHAMPIONS

"My Lords," Phoena cried. "Please don't kneel before me. I'm only a servant." She reached out towards each of them, trying to persuade them to rise. She was careful not to be too familiar – not daring to touch them. "Karilion, you mustn't... Baraapa, surely you are the sensible one... Oramis, please..."

A shadow fell over the tableau.

Phoena flinched. Lord Westernbrooke and Matron were standing a few paces away.

It took but a moment for the girl to drag herself upright. This was more than enough time to regret parting with her overdress. In slow motion, the jacket Baraapa had draped over her body drifted to the ground. The damp petticoat clung to her slender figure.

A stiff breeze blew along the riverbank, and she shivered as she considered retrieving the jacket. Then this idea faded, replaced by a throbbing pain in her head which warned against any sudden movement. That pain behind her eyes flashed in rhythm with a tingling in her fingers and toes.

The temptation to drop back into nothingness grew.

If she had been alone, she might have yielded to the darkness at the edge of her mind. Phoena dragged her eyes towards the young noblemen. They no longer knelt before her. With a shout, they leapt to their feet as a team. With their bodies between her and the new arrivals, the trio drew their swords.

The air resounded with the song of tensile steel ripped from the safety of scabbards by enthusiastic youths.

"So that's how it will be," Lord Westernbrooke said. His massive arm began to rise, and the air around him glimmered as his power surged.

"NO!" screamed Phoena.

Without thought, the maid raised her hands in the air.

Three swords clattered onto the grass in front of her as her would-be defenders soared over her head. The ground shook as they landed behind her. Their outraged complaints revealed how far she had thrown them. Her pain intensified, and her whole body complained that she had overextended her reach. But there was no time to reflect on her actions. Already, the young noblemen had scrambled to their feet, loudly declaring their intentions to defend her, regardless of the cost.

This was not the time to be timid. She lurched forward to meet Lord Westernbrooke. "You must not harm them!"

"You dare to challenge me?"

With her eyes fixed on his angry face, Phoena became a statue. Was that what she was doing? Challenging his authority? How did she come to this ridiculous situation? A half-drowned orphan-girl giving orders to one of the senior nobility.

And yet – his hand stilled. The threatening cloud of power that had surrounded Lord Westernbrooke faded. He stood far enough away that she did not feel threatened by his presence. But now his eyes took in her appearance. Phoena glanced down. The blood drained from her face. A water-soaked petticoat was a most unsatisfactory covering. She shuffled her bare feet.

At that moment, as if it were her only concern, stinging pain on her arm demanded her full attention. What was the stickiness where her fingers pressed against her goose-bumped skin? An answer came. This must be where the fish hook had wounded her.

Matron took a step closer, removing the white shawl she was wearing and offering it to Phoena. The shivering girl reached for it, and Matron dropped it into her hands. The maid wrapped herself in the still-warm garment. Matron peered into Phoena's eyes for a moment and nodded, before returning to her position beside Lord Westernbrooke.

As Matron withdrew, Karilion appeared at Phoena's left side. Oramis stood by her right. Their hands retrieved their unsheathed swords. She glanced at them. They were far enough from her that they could wield their weapons without striking her.

Lord Westernbrooke's frown darkened.

"Your pardon, My Lady," Baraapa whispered in her ear. His hand appeared on her shoulder. She gasped. Could he sense the heat that his touch had awoken within her? It felt as if her shoulder was on fire. He stiffened. "Please forgive this liberty, but we can't risk you disappearing alone."

His fingers trembled. Phoena reached up and touched his hand. A blast of white-hot pain exploded in her chest. She jerked her hand, but with a twist of his wrist, he held her fingers captive against her shoulder. They stared at each other.

The concern on Baraapa's face deepened. He shuffled closer.

"Uh-hum." Lord Westernbrooke sounded even more annoyed. Matron put her hand on Lord Westernbrooke's arm and shook her head.

"We agreed," Matron said to him, "that *this* time we would do things *my* way. You can't help yourself, but when you play headmaster with the child, you frighten her too much."

"I frighten her!" he roared. "I'm sure I've aged a hundred years since she first disappeared."

"And you're doing *nothing* to improve the situation by shouting." Matron continued as if she were lecturing one of the footmen. "She is not one of your troublesome boys. When I agreed to come to the *Academy*, you didn't tell me you intended to remove yourself from the scene. I would have advised against it. A lot has happened in fourteen years."

"I suppose you're right, Cecily." Lord Westernbrooke rubbed his forehead. A sheepish smile appeared on his face. "You usually are. I'll leave the talking to you."

Phoena stared. She had never heard anyone address Matron by any other name. And Matron-Cecily spoke to the intimidating man as if she was his equal. There was a special bond here that spoke of a deeper mystery.

This domineering woman had been difficult to please, always lurking in the background. Ready to step forward to deliver a reprimand. A thousand questions sprang into the maid's mind, as Phoena re-evaluated Matron's presence in significant situations.

She wrestled the questions into silence. The effort made Phoena stagger. Baraapa pressed his body against her, slipping his other arm around her waist. She offered a half-smile.

Lord Westernbrooke spoke again. "Cecily, please tell that young man to remove his hands from my goddaughter. And make those fools put away their swords."

His words only heightened the tension. Phoena prayed that the young men would overlook their wounded pride. She doubted her ability to throw them to safety again.

Lord Westernbrooke behaved like a first-year student called to explain himself to Matron. "I shouldn't have consented to the release of their swords from the Armoury. I only did so because of the reports of local brigands at work nearby. I never expected the young cockatiels to use their weapons against me."

"The young 'cockatiels' are the newest members of the Fellowship," Matron said. "You would do well to remember that."

"Cecily, confirmation about their membership is not final," Lord Westernbrooke replied.

"Westy, that's piffle, and you know it." Cecily put her hands on her hips, frowned and waggled a finger at him.

"Have you forgotten I was there at *your* membership confirmation?"

She waved her other hand at the young noblemen. "You already know that their nominations are accepted and ratified. Any other business with the Fellowship is but a formality. You should be thankful that they've only drawn their swords. There's no telling what your goddaughter has done to their powers."

A different expression appeared on Lord

Westernbrooke's face. Now he looked more like the headmaster in the portrait in the *Academy* hallway. "I'll send them through the assessment examination again."

"No, you won't!" Karilion cried. "I'm not an untrained child. Why should I submit to another examination? Nothing has happened to my magic."

Phoena's headache intensified. Only Baraapa's support kept her on her feet. His chest was hot against her chilled shoulders.

"Hmmph." Lord Westernbrooke glowered at Karilion. He addressed Cecily. "Full of hot air, this one. No need to question which of the domains he represents."

"Oh-ho," laughed Oramis. "Karilion, he has your measure."

"And you," Lord Westernbrooke said to Oramis, "are more smoke and illusion than fire. You haven't distinguished yourself either, but you will have to do."

"If neither of us impresses you," Karilion said. "I dread to hear what you make of poor Baraapa. This unlikely hero has no magic. He's neither water nor earth. But our scientific rationalist keeps the rest of us grounded."

Baraapa stiffened behind her. "This is all very interesting, but you seem to have forgotten that Her Ladyship is unwell."

Another wave of dizziness threatened Phoena. Her body was too heavy to support itself. She slid towards the ground. Poor Baraapa dropped to his knees, unable to hold her.

An uncomfortable silence followed his words. Baraapa struggled alone. He grappled with Phoena's leaden weight as she wrestled with this new puzzle. She had become accustomed to everyone reaching for her with their hands.

So why were they keeping their distance now? Was it her imagination, or did even Lord Westernbrooke take a step backwards?

"What's wrong?" Baraapa asked, finally managing to scoop her up into his arms. The small nobleman pulled her towards his chest. Every muscle strained with the load as he staggered to his feet.

Oramis spoke first. "Her powers are still awakening."

"Why is that a problem?"

"It might not be safe to magic her anywhere."

"It took her three days to find her way back this time, and look at the state of her," Karilion reminded Baraapa.

"If we lose her again while she's this weak," Matron said, "she might not survive."

"Ah!" Baraapa said, nodding as he looked from face to face. He turned to Oramis. "Change into your dragon form. It will only take a few minutes to fly her back to the Academy."

"Umm." Oramis scuffed the ground with his boots. "It might not be safe to touch her in my magical form, either."

"What?" Baraapa screamed. "All my life, I've envied you magic-users, and now you're as helpless as me." Words flew from him like lightning in a thunderstorm. "You're more concerned about your own safety than her wellbeing. I can see how it is. It's up to me again."

They backed away. He pushed through the gap towards the road. "I'll carry her then. It's going to take longer without help. Use that time well. Magic yourselves back but make sure you've thought of some way to help her before we arrive."

"I'm staying with you," Karilion said.

"So am I," Oramis declared. "Matron can send a coach to meet us. We can't help carry her, but we'll be with you in case anyone accosts you on the road."

CHAPTER 16:
AN UNLIKELY HERO

With her head turned towards Baraapa's chest, Phoena took comfort from his tight embrace. But she worried that such close contact was doing him harm. His torso twitched as if some kind of spasm was rippling through his body. He walked in silence. Her heart pounded erratically. Eventually, it settled to match the tempo of his feet.

She almost forgot the two noblemen who walked behind them. When Oramis and Karilion raised their voices, some of their words tickled her ears.

"Why did you protest so vehemently about being tested again?" Oramis asked. He sounded near.

"For the same reason you didn't want to be tested," Karilion said.

"I never—"

"Deny it all you like. I saw your sword hand twitch. You don't want them to know the full extent of your magical capabilities either."

"I've been trained all my life to hide, diminish and conceal," Oramis said. "But I thought someone like you, Karilion, would want to show off your power to anyone who expressed the slightest interest."

"Do you think me that shallow?"

"Perhaps not," Oramis conceded.

"I didn't want to arrive at the King's Council and have everyone know my strengths and weaknesses."

"I've always suspected there were complex layers under that pretty-boy exterior," Oramis said. "I didn't want to test my theory, because I would have to report back to my superiors. Why do you think I deliberately set out to alienate you upon my arrival?"

"Aha. I knew I was your principal assignment," Karilion cried.

Oramis laughed. "Your imminent ascent to the King's Council at such a young age makes you the obvious target. I never cared for the plan. There have to be better ways of gaining intelligence from neighbouring countries than trying to befriend the underage heirs."

"You're older than you said."

"Only by a few years," Oramis conceded. "You should be thankful that I took this assignment, or they would have sent my younger brother instead. He would have given you a run for your money with the ladies."

"Are you married?"

"Of course not. I wouldn't have accepted your challenge for My Lady's affection if I wasn't free to accept her favours when I win."

"You haven't won yet!"

"I'm thinking that neither of us is making as much progress as Viscount Baraapa."

"You've changed the subject," Karilion declared.

"How have I done that?"

"We were talking about how our talent has changed since we were tested as children. But I'm thinking there have been more significant changes since we met *her*."

Phoena grew even more still. She desperately wanted to hear that the other noblemen were unchanged.

The muscles in Baraapa's arms were hardening, as they squeezed her tight. His breathing slowed, and she guessed he was trying to eavesdrop on the conversation too.

"*She* has a name," Oramis said.

"I know, but you're just as loath to speak it as the rest of us."

"Why do you think I should be reluctant?"

"There's power in the use of a personal name," Karilion said.

"More so," Oramis agreed, "now that we've caught a glimpse of how much power she has at her disposal."

"But how can we be sure we even know her name?"

"She told us her name is Phoena," Oramis said.

"I know," Karilion said, "but Lord Westernbrooke called her Lady Firebird."

"Which is why I'm certain that what she told us is true." Oramis left the words hanging there. "He also talked about a Fellowship."

"You know something."

"So would you," Oramis said, "if you hadn't been daydreaming through your philosophy classes. Every master I've known has relied on the tale of the legendary Elemental Fellowship to explain our cultural alliances. The master you have here did so yesterday."

"Well, I didn't know it was going to be significant to me personally, so I didn't take notes," Karilion said. "Tell me what I missed."

For a few minutes, the two noblemen exchanged insults. Phoena feared she would never hear about the Fellowship. A tear rolled down her cheek.

Oramis was the first one to moderate his tone. "There's an ancient legend about a Fellowship – five champions on a righteous quest. Each of the elements was represented by a champion, and the fifth man, who was their leader, had the full complement. He was the first one to be described as an 'elemental virtuoso'. He could shape-shift to the form of a phoenix–"

"Phoe– But she– Surely not?" Karilion asked.

"How old do you think she is?"

"You've changed the subject again," Karilion muttered. "What does her age have to do with anything? Unless you're suggesting that she's hundreds of years old. Is she the first leader, reincarnated?"

"Of course not," Oramis said. "Every version of the legend agrees that the phoenix shape-shifter was mortal. He aged like the rest of them – grew old – and died. There's a monument to him and his successor in the Thristian Mountains. If my guess is correct, she's a direct descendant. I asked you about her age because you're more knowledgeable about women."

"When we first met her," Karilion said, "I thought she was in her twenties, one of those plain women who might never attract a husband. But now that some of the magical defences have lifted, I'd say she's much younger, maybe sixteen or seventeen. Why do you ask?"

"Matron said Phoena's been here fourteen years, which matches with other information I have accumulated. 'Fourteen years' is a memorable phrase, like 'a year and a day' in Baraapa's fairy tale. I remember details like that. I find them exceedingly helpful in uncovering patterns and revealing secrets."

"Get on with it," Karilion muttered. Phoena heard what sounded like a scuffle.

"Oi! Keep your hands to yourself," Oramis complained. "There's no need to shove me. I was merely filling in the gaps in your education."

"And I'm reminding *you* I'm not a pawn in your game. We're supposed to be working together for this *Fellowship*."

"I can't argue with your logic," Oramis said. "Fourteen years ago, Lord Westernbrooke mysteriously disappeared from the *Academy*. He was gone for a few weeks, and upon his return, he announced his unexpected retirement. His replacement was installed immediately. By *coincidence*, Matron was appointed at the same time."

There was another long pause.

"And now you're going to tell me you know where Lord Westernbrooke went," Karilion said.

"I want you to swear not to tell anyone else. If I'm right, there was a reason they kept her existence a secret. We need to be careful until we know what that reason was."

"Finally, something we both agree on. I promise to keep your secret, so tell me what you know."

"Many years ago," Oramis said, "a rumour from the outer realms reached the Emberite capital. It was a tale about a widow, who lived somewhere in the remotest mountains."

"The Thristian mountains?" Karilion asked. "Is that why you think she's a descendant?"

"Not the Thristian mountains. Another mountain range in the opposite direction. As far away as it would be possible to go, and still be within civilised lands. Let me continue with my story. This widow was rarely seen but from *intelligence* gathered afterwards, she must have been there for several years before tragedy befell her."

"You've checked this out yourself?" Karilion asked.

Phoena held her breath and waited. The silence lengthened. Baraapa continued forward, but she could sense his tension increasing with each step. When Oramis spoke again, that nobleman seemed to have fallen further behind.

"Once a month, on market day, the widow would come down from the mountains. There were a handful of settlements in the region, and she never visited the same village two months in a row. She came for a purpose and never tarried. Nor did she bring anything to sell. Yet the widow always had money to spend. The few merchants she frequented were well paid, and she gave them extra coin if they demonstrated respect for her privacy.

"Then one market day, fourteen years ago, she appeared in the same village a second time. Her clothes were blackened, and she was in great distress. She babbled about a burning child. No one had ever suspected there might be a child living with the widow, so the curious villagers hurried to her home.

"Nothing remained of her cottage. Even the bricks of the chimney had crumbled in the heat from an intense blaze. They looked for a body but found no bones among the rubble. A search was conducted of the whole area, but apart from a single set of small footprints by the river, no trace of a child was ever found.

"A few days later," Oramis continued, "an intimidating giant with a flowing white beard arrived in the village. He carried a silver-topped staff. This man took rooms in the inn and then summoned the widow. She was ushered in to see him. When the landlord came to inquire if there was anything they needed, there was no sign of either of them. The widow was never seen again."

"You think *she's* that child," Karilion said. "You think the poor widow didn't realise the child was fire-adept so when she ignited—"

"We already know that she transports herself somewhere safe when she's afraid," Oramis said. "So, while she was on fire, she took herself away. I think Lord Westernbrooke waited for her return and captured her."

"But that happened fourteen years ago," Karilion said. "How could so much time pass without further incident? Unless... Oh!"

"Exactly. Somebody suppressed her powers. She must have been young when it happened, for her to forget that she had so great a power."

Oramis paused. "I don't think Lord Westernbrooke could bear to see the fragile waif she became without her power. That's why he left so suddenly."

"Fourteen years is a long time to live without magic," Karilion said. "She was hidden in plain sight among the untalented servants. When we encountered her that first day, there was nothing in her appearance that marked her as special. I remember thinking she wasn't pretty enough to warrant a second glance."

"But you did take a second glance. Have you wondered about that? There's another thing that's puzzled me. That day I expected you to be gone all morning. What made you come back to your room?"

"Baraapa's companions activated my defensive wards while they were searching for you. I came back to catch a thief."

"You wouldn't have anything I'd want," Oramis insisted.

"What were you doing in my room then?"

"I've already told you," Oramis said. "I went to your room searching for an unknown adversary. Ironically, the defences designed to hide her presence were the only reason I found her. The harder I pushed, the stronger the reaction against me. That mysterious influence was more intense than anything I had encountered before.

"Even non-magic Baraapa could sense that power. Once I knew it was coming from your room, I redirected all my energy. I wanted to ensure I survived long enough to identify the source. I took myself beyond my known limitations.

"The restrictive magic over-stretched itself, keeping me contained while trying to deal with Baraapa's physical threat. Then you walked in, and everything began to unravel."

"What are you saying?" Karilion asked.

"I think her unfathomable talent called to each of us," Oramis said, "including Baraapa, long before we knew she existed. Her power sought us out because it needed all three of us. We acted as the catalyst for her release. That is how we were nominated for the Fellowship."

"And how did we accept?"

"We chased after the mystery and pieced together some of the puzzle pieces," Oramis said, "and then when we understood who she was, we bowed before her."

There was a long pause. "What happens next?"

"We change and adapt to meet her requirements," Oramis said.

"I don't want to change," Karilion said.

"Neither do I. My life was mapped out and now everything is uncertain. I was happy to be a shape-shifting black and red dragon with big plans, but now I think I'll become a red and black dragon with bigger plans."

Karilion laughed. "There's no difference, you crazy Emberite."

"I assure you," Oramis chuckled, "there's a world of difference. Now put aside your worries about the future and let's catch up to Baraapa. Instead of tiring, he seems to have increased his speed."

CHAPTER 17:
THE PRICE FOR CHIVALRY

Baraapa jostled Phoena to adjust his grip, and she sighed. She turned her head towards his face. He gazed at her and then she knew.

"You do have magic," she whispered. "You have to put me down."

He shook his head. She didn't have time to ask whether he was denying his magic, or if he was saying that it was too late to stop whatever was happening.

"Stand and deliver!" a strange voice shouted.

Phoena twisted her head. She caught a glimpse of a thin, scruffy man, waving a pistol. He had a strip of brown cloth wrapped around his face, and a wide black hat pulled low on his brow.

Baraapa guided her eyes back to his chest and stepped from the road. It felt as if he was retreating towards the trees that bordered the lane.

"Stand and deliver?" Karilion cried, leaping forward with his sword drawn. "Is that the best line you can come up with? Ho! Prepare to defend yourself."

The swish of a blade sang in the air. Then a shot rang out. "Ha! You missed," Karilion cried. "What good is a pistol if you miss with your first shot?"

Something landed on the ground close by, then a smoking pistol appeared near Baraapa's feet.

Oramis joined the fray with a shout. "What, are there only six of you? And only one pistol. The rest of you have knives. That hardly seems like a fair fight."

"Put me down," Phoena insisted. The power was building within her. "There are six of them. Karilion and Oramis are going to be killed."

"And what do you think you can do about that, my pretty?" asked another voice.

Baraapa stiffened.

There were two more ruffians hidden among the trees. A rough hand gripped her chin, and then cruel eyes stared at her face. "There's a rich ransom to be had for you, sweetheart," the bandit said, and he licked his lips. "Come along, my pretty. If you don't put up a fight, we might let your friends live to boast about their bravery."

A knife blade waved towards Baraapa's face. He squeezed her tight. "Eight stones in the river."

The ground beneath Phoena's feet rumbled, and Baraapa fell to his knees. She tumbled roughly from his arms and rolled across the ground. When the ringing in her ears subsided, she saw fashionable boots appear beside her.

"What happened?" Karilion asked. "Where did the bandits go? I didn't need anyone's help. I was winning."

"Answers," Phoena croaked, her forehead dropping back to the grass. The gilded frame of the mystical mirror pressed into her hand. She thrust it towards Karilion as her eyes closed.

"O-ho!" Karilion cried. "You put them in the river."

"Let me see," Oramis said, and then he began to laugh. "See how deep it is and how swift the water flows. They will be in a sad and sorry state by the time they make their way back to land. Plenty of time for us to get away to safety."

"How did she do that?"

"Ask her yourself."

"Stop talking about me," Phoena said, taking a deep breath and lifting her head, "as if I wasn't here. Baraapa and I worked together. 'Eight stones in the river'."

"What do you mean you worked together?" Oramis asked. "You and Baraapa? But—"

Karilion swore.

"Help me," Phoena demanded.

Oramis held out a broken branch. When she took hold of one end, he hoisted her to her knees. She crawled to Baraapa, who lay unconscious on the ground. His whole body was humming and buzzing with brilliant orange light.

"Don't touch him," Oramis said. "Let the magic sort itself

out."

"Does magic take care of itself?"

Oramis frowned at her and then shrugged. "I'm beginning to think your kind might."

"But he didn't have any magic," Karilion said. "His father insisted that he go for reassessment at the start of each semester, in case he was late developing his talent. This week's results were unchanged."

"He might have had no magic before," Oramis said, "but there's no denying he has a healthy dose now."

"Why has the skin on his hand changed colour?" Phoena asked. "It looks like the reddish clay from the riverbank."

Oramis leaned closer. "Is that the hand he used to clear the mud from your mouth when you were having trouble breathing?"

"That's the same hand he put on your shoulder," Karilion said, "when we confronted your godfather. I saw you cover it with your hand as you smiled at him. I remember thinking he'd outfoxed us again."

"Show us your hands," Oramis said.

Phoena obeyed.

Oramis leaned closer and pointed. "There's blood on your fingers. Are you bleeding?"

She searched for the wound on her arm and showed it to him. "This is where the fish hook cut me before it broke free and snagged onto my petticoat. It's stopped bleeding now, but it still hurts."

Oramis rolled the unconscious Viscount over. "Hmm." He fell silent. There was a bloody patch on the front of Baraapa's white shirt, where he had held her against his chest.

"What?" Karilion said impatiently. "I thought we agreed not to keep any secrets from each other."

"We were worried about even touching her, but Baraapa is covered in her blood. That shouldn't have affected him, since everyone agreed that Baraapa had no magic. But what if the tests weren't calibrated properly?"

"What do you mean?"

"Baraapa has a reputation for being skilled with mechanical things. Where the rest of us rely on magic, he uses tools to achieve his goals. I know there's nobody at the *Academy* who is better than him at opening locks."

"Tools and locks?" Karilion asked. "There's nothing magic about them. We already know he's clever. How is this relevant?"

"Did we give him any credit for the role he played in today's rescue?" Oramis asked. "Fishing was his idea. I watched the joy on his face as he set up his equipment. I didn't recognise it for the physical energy it was, because it wasn't the kind of power I'm used to. I dismissed it as some kind of emotional compensation for his lack of talent. He was especially careful with the selection of his hook."

"You think he knew he was going to catch her in the river?"

"Karilion, don't you listen to anything I say?" Oramis asked. "All the key decisions we've made in this adventure have been because *her* power has called to us."

"You're telling me Baraapa's decision to use that particular hook was because his magic wanted to join with hers?"

"I'm not sure I like the way you phrased that," Oramis grumbled. "Think about it. I jumped in the river, and afterwards, I wondered what I was doing there. And you started pelting the river with rocks. You were getting closer and closer to the water. I expected you to fall in at any moment. All three of us were being called towards her, and each of us played a part in her recovery."

"The magic humming has stopped," Karilion said, "and I can hear the coach. Is it safe to move Baraapa now?"

They watched the vehicle approach. Four well matched chestnut horses pulled the the enclosed coach. It had an upper luggage rack, and a bench seat at the rear, as well as seating inside. The *Westernbrooke Academy* crest decorated the door.

There was only one man at the reins, and he wore the uniform of an *Academy* stableman.

"Lord Karilion," he cried, bringing the coach to a standstill beside them. "Matron didn't tell me which young lords I was to retrieve. Why am I not surprised to find you amid some melodrama? From the cut on your cheek and those rips in your jacket, it looks as if you've been fighting again."

Karilion smiled. "Hampton, I'm pleased to see that it's you. We've just fought off a band of robbers. I'd be thankful if you didn't pass that information on to Matron. She would bring down a curfew. Of course, I'll reward you handsomely when we get back."

"Matron has already promised me a reward," Hampton replied, as he sprang down from the driver's seat. "I am especially commanded to forget that I've seen this young lady." He opened the door and reached inside. "Matron sent a thick woollen cloak to make the young lady's journey more *comfortable.*"

"When you've wrapped the cloak around her, Hampton, could you please help Her Ladyship into the coach?"

Hampton paused, a speculative look on his face. "It's not like you, My Lord, to pass up an opportunity to provide the *assistance* yourself."

Karilion slipped his hand into his pocket. "If you knew the name of Her Ladyship's guardian," he said, producing a silver coin, "you'd understand my discretion. I have no desire to be exiled."

Hampton accepted the coin with a nod and slipped it into his pocket.

"My Lady, please allow me to help you into the coach," Hampton said to Phoena, and he quickly organised her transfer.

"Thank you." Phoena leaned against the inside of the coach, and Hampton tucked the long cloak snugly around her. Karilion stuck his head through the open doorway and grinned at her.

"What about Baraapa?" she asked.

"Now that you're settled, Oramis and I will drag him over. Ordinarily, I'd tell Oramis to carry him by himself, but our unconscious friend is no longer a lightweight."

Phoena frowned. Karilion and Oramis strained to raise their companion from the ground. Hampton hurried to assist.

The three of them half-dragged, half-lifted the unconscious man into the carriage. When Baraapa had been bundled onto the seat opposite Phoena, Oramis sat beside him to keep him from tumbling to the floor.

As soon as the door closed, Karilion jumped onto the external running board and wrapped his arm around the door support. Hampton assumed the driver's seat, and the coach began to move.

Leaning forward, Phoena studied Baraapa. He was larger all over. Even slumped in his seat. he towered over Oramis.

Baraapa's face had changed. It seemed more angular, and his skin glowed as if it were dusted with copper. His hair was now bright orange. His hands had doubled in size. Those fists looked as if they could crush rocks into gravel without effort.

The seams of his shirt had ripped during the transfer, and firm muscles bulged through the gaps. Her eyes followed his form to his feet. Like the rest of him, his legs were powerfully made.

The only other person she had ever seen with such well-defined muscles was the village blacksmith. Phoena remembered visiting the smithy with Heilga. Was it only a fortnight ago? Her friend had lingered to admire the bare-chested man at work. Heilga had laughed at Phoena's shyness. The blacksmith had ignored Phoena, content to bask in Heilga's adoration.

And Heilga had not been the only one to smile prettily towards the man. A steady flow of young women had passed by. Afterwards, Heilga had talked about nothing except the blacksmith for the rest of the day.

Uncomfortable with where her thoughts were leading, Phoena wondered how Baraapa would respond to the changes. She already knew how the chambermaids would react. Would he be happy with the extra attention?

Karilion coughed. "It would seem that Her Ladyship is fascinated by Baraapa's transformation."

Phoena blushed.

"How are you going to explain what has happened to him?" she asked, averting her eyes.

"Oramis will think of something. My contribution will be to summon my tailor so the Viscount can acquire a wardrobe more suited to his new body."

"I've come to the conclusion that Baraapa is the earth element," Oramis said.

"Your reasoning?" Karilion asked.

"Apart from his rock-like muscles?" Oramis winked at Phoena. "I told you he was good with tools and locks. They're all made of metal. I'm thinking he's had some minor metal-affinity all along."

"That could explain why he's the second-best swordsman at the *Academy*," Karilion said. "I've always wondered why no-one else could defeat him."

"Second only to you?" Oramis asked. "I look forward to seeing you bested when he comes into his full strength."

Karilion frowned. Phoena closed her eyes for a moment. When she opened them again, Oramis was studying her. He leaned towards Karilion. "We should be considering where to look for the water-affinity champion."

"There's another champion?" Karilion asked. "It hardly seems fair to have another man join the contest at this late stage."

"What do you think, My Lady?" Oramis said with a grin. "Have you been entertaining any other noblemen that we know nothing about?"

"You talk such nonsense," Phoena said.

"I agree," said Karilion. "What would she want with another nobleman, when she has us to choose from? You're spouting nothing but nonsense."

Oramis pouted. "Of course, I dare not argue with her Ladyship." His eyes twinkled with the hint of red flame. She leaned back into the furthest corner and frowned at him.

He nodded. "It's good to see that her Ladyship has not

forgotten the serious nature of our situation. Though having seen what her power did to Baraapa, I'm tempted–"

"No!" Karilion shouted, reaching in the window. He pressed Oramis against the back of his seat. "One unconscious changeling is sufficient for today."

"I agree," Phoena said. Beads of perspiration appeared on her forehead.

Oramis looked from one companion to the other. He tilted his head and grinned. "This afternoon has been very informative."

"You were telling us where we should look for the fourth champion," Karilion said.

"So, I was. I'm a hundred percent certain if the water-affinity champion was anywhere nearby, they would have been pulled into her Ladyship's enchantment along with the rest of us."

A leather whip lightly flicked Karilion's shoulder. He leaned back out the window and said something to Hampton. Despite the open window, Phoena heard nothing.

"A handy little anti-eavesdropping spell," Oramis said. "Silver or no silver, I don't know whether Hampton can be trusted. Make sure you pull up the hood on your cloak when you get out of the coach."

Phoena nodded.

Karilion leaned back in. "We're almost at the entrance to the northern wing. I can see Lord Westernbrooke standing on the steps. Oramis, if you have anything to tell us, you'd better be quick."

"It is obvious that the water-affinity champion is somewhere else." Oramis folded his arms across his chest and refused to be drawn into further conversation.

CHAPTER 18:
THE COACH ARRIVES

Oramis and Karilion stepped back while Hampton lifted Phoena from the carriage. She saw the pair talking with Lord Westernbrooke as the coachman carried her away.

Matron waited at the top of the stairs. Without comment, the woman entered the hallway, and Hampton followed a few paces behind. They passed along the flagstone hallway to the second guest apartment.

An unfamiliar footman stood at the open double doors. Cecily nodded, and he removed Phoena from Hampton's arms. The footman tarried in the hallway while Matron spoke with the coachman.

"Thank you, Hampton," the older woman said. "Please accept this token for the service you provided this day."

Hampton received the leather pouch with a wide smile. He bowed before retreating the way he came. Phoena's eyes followed the coachman. The coins clinked in his hand as he walked.

Oramis stood in the doorway, waiting until Hampton had left before he approached.

The blond nobleman jerked his head towards the door. "Are you sure you can trust Hampton?"

"What silver can't achieve, a forgetfulness spell will do," Cecily replied. "Why aren't you in the coach with the others?"

"Lord Westernbrooke decided to accompany Baraapa. It will take some time to explain the situation to Nurse. There wasn't any room for me in the coach with that senior nobleman taking up a whole seat. I said I would make my own way back."

Cecily nodded to the footman, who stepped across the threshold into the guest apartment. He carried Phoena through the reception room to the master bedroom.

Oramis followed, in close step with Cecily. "I see you've recruited a new footman. I should warn you that even non-magicals are at risk when her Ladyship has a crisis."

"I've already prepared for that possibility," Cecily said, blocking the doorway, and preventing Oramis from entering the bedchamber. "Go and attend to Viscount Baraapa. Your presence is not needed here."

The footman delivered Phoena to a sofa and retreated towards the door. An unknown noblewoman, dressed entirely in silvery grey from head to toe, was waiting beside the sofa. Her complexion was dark, and there was something about her features that reminded the teenager of the ailing Viscount.

This woman was broad-shouldered and even taller than the intimidating Matron. There was the same kind of authority in the way she held herself. Her clothes were the same colour as the grey hair piled high upon her head. Elaborate ringlets fell beside her ears, which were adorned with silvery pearl earrings.

The lace at the woman's neck and cuffs was exquisitely crafted, and the fabric of her dress was much finer than any Phoena had ever seen. The air around this woman had the aroma of garden flowers after a refreshing spring rain. A delicate swish accompanied every movement.

She began to remove the cloak. Phoena whimpered, flapping her arms without effect. She had no strength to defend herself from the unwelcome attention.

"Shhh," the woman whispered, and then she smiled. Phoena's heart leapt at the affection that shone from the stranger's eyes. A warmed blanket replaced her cloak before the grey-haired woman turned away to the fire.

Phoena refocused her attention on the doorway, where Oramis was still trying to force his way past the footman.

"I'll not leave," Oramis said. "Not until I have your assurance that you won't steal away her Ladyship without a proper farewell."

"We both know that it's not safe for her to travel," Cecily said. "Should that change, I'll let you know. Now leave, before I have you removed."

The footman seemed to grow in stature, and he stepped closer to the young nobleman. Phoena gasped. The woman in grey was beside her in an instant. She took hold of the girl's hand and squeezed it with her own.

"There, there, Shurma," the woman crooned with an unfamiliar accent. "Time enough for that when you're rested."

Oramis raised his voice as the door began to close in his face. "Please let her Ladyship know that I go with great reluctance and that I will await her next summons."

"Go, you foolish boy," Cecily said. She gave him a small shove. The footman followed the young nobleman, closing the door behind him with a bang. With the door shut, all sound from outside the bedchamber ceased. There was a flicker of magical light around the door frame. Phoena's eyes flew to the heavy curtains that covered the windows.

Cecily came towards Phoena's sofa. "That one is persistent. Do not worry about Oramis or the others. Focus now on regaining your strength."

"Yes, Matron."

"Call me Cecily. Our time in this place nears an end. I will soon put off this disguise."

Phoena opened her mouth to ask a question, but Cecily shushed her. "Your questions can wait. I'm going to leave you with Lady Ennallya. She is more gentle and patient than I. She knows what you need. Lie still. Let her bathe you, and tend to your wounds. I'll return when you're settled."

Without another word, Cecily left through the door. The teenager stared after her. The woman in grey hummed a tune as she continued her preparations. A cake of fragrant lavender soap and a pile of towels were placed beside her sofa.

The helpless girl could not even raise her hand, so there was no choice but to submit to this stranger's ministrations. Phoena couldn't remember ever having anyone help her bathe. Lady Ennallya carried over a large basin filled with hot water and then began removing Phoena's ruined petticoat. The girl closed her eyes, embarrassment giving way to tears.

"Hush, hush, Shurma," the woman said. "You've been in the river. Black and blue you'll be on the morrow." As she talked, the soft washcloth moved over Phoena's body. "It's a blessing that there are but one or two wounds that need a poultice. There's no need to risk magic here. Don't you worry, Shurma. Old Ennallya knows the herbal remedies from the ancient days."

Phoena had a dozen questions. "You don't look old."

Lady Ennallya laughed. "I'm old enough to have seen ten kings come and go. I was old before your grandmother was born. And I hope to live long enough to see your grandchildren brought into the world."

"You knew my grandmother?"

"Shh, Shurma. There will be time enough for answers after your body has healed."

"Why do you call me 'Shurma'?"

"That's the name your grandmother preferred when she was a girl. You remind me a little of her. She also had the river in her soul. On more than one occasion, *she* needed rescuing from the river."

After Lady Ennallya wrapped Phoena in warm towels, it was time to wash and comb the tangled hair.

"I've seen many marvels in my time," Lady Ennallya said. "But I've never seen hair like yours. Now that it is wet, I can smell the damp earth of my homeland. It reminds me of how the soil rejoices after heavy rain."

Phoena lay back against the padded chair, pondering how to respond, as Lady Ennallya braided the brown-black hair. Next, she attended to the wounds from the river ordeal. The place where the fish hook had torn Phoena's arm received the most attention. It was angry and red.

"This one will leave a scar," Lady Ennallya said. "Another reminder of the transformation you are going through."

"I'm not finished changing?" Phoena cried.

"You have eyes like the river, and hair like the earth. There's still fire and air to leave their mark. You will be memorable when the transformation is complete. After you reach your maturity, you will have more than one man eager to claim your heart."

"She already has three suitors," Cecily said, announcing her return. Phoena hadn't heard the door open or close. "Her godfather is determined to keep them from advancing their claims."

"I sense this maid is more independent than her predecessors," Lady Ennallya laughed. "When she makes her choice, Westy will have a battle on his hands. He will find it impossible to stop the tide of love. It would be easier if her guardian turned his efforts to dissuading the moon from rising."

"I will bow to your wisdom and experience, Ennallya," Cecily said. "By the time her father started listening to his heart, it was already too late. All that political posturing and manoeuvring was a disaster in the making. You and I must work to ensure history doesn't repeat itself."

"Help me get her onto the bed," Ennallya said.

Phoena was firmly tucked beneath the covers of the four-poster bed. The two women whispered together near the fire. Cecily held an earthenware beaker. Ennallya poured hot water into the mug and stirred the brew using a green-leafed twig.

Ennallya raised Phoena's head from the pillow while Cecily offered the teenager the steaming brew.

"Herbs from the mountains," Ennallya said, "to make your body sleep."

The steam wafted over Phoena's face, and her eyes began to water. The liquid burned her tongue, and the bitterness made her gag. Ennallya's grip was both strong and relentless. As with the other ministrations, Phoena was helpless to resist. The girl swallowed, and the rest of the herbal concoction was quickly consumed.

She lay back on the pillows, staring up at the ruffled canopy. Her chest was tight, making it difficult to breathe. A strange heaviness pressed against her forehead. She shook her head in an attempt to be free of it.

"Don't fight it," Ennallya said. "Close your eyes. I will sing you a song to help you find your peace."

A lifetime of obedience robbed Phoena of any further resistance. She closed her eyes. The words were in a foreign tongue, but Ennallya's tune seemed familiar.

"Hide me now," Phoena murmured the words of her childhood prayer, as she drifted to sleep.

The words of the song haunted her dreams.

CHAPTER 19:
FAREWELL DREAMER

A peace that was deeper and stronger than she had ever imagined wrapped itself around Phoena. She floated in sparkling blue water, rocked by the waves. Her face was towards the sky as the sun dipped below the horizon. Grey clouds were transformed with vivid strokes of violet and crimson.

Night followed day.

A thousand twinkling stars, high above in the navy blue night sky, echoed the song:

Shaezz vraa moem neis.

Time passed...
The light show faded.

Her ears detected a whispered conversation, but she was unable to open her eyes. The speaker drew nearer.

"As you can see," Lady Ennallya said, "she still sleeps."

"Thank you for allowing me to see for myself," Oramis said. "I've been petitioning Matron for the past three days, but she's shown me no mercy."

"Then it is fortunate for you that Cecily has been called away."

Phoena felt a light touch to the side of her face. She knew without needing her sight that Oramis must be standing there. The heat from his hand lingered long after his fingers were snatched away.

"Please do not try to wake her," Lady Ennallya said.

"I don't think that would be possible," he said. "There is powerful magic at work here."

"It is all her own. We only gave her a herbal draught to help her sleep; then I sang prayers and petitions over her until she settled. Her spirit has taken command of the healing."

"How long will she sleep?" Oramis asked.

"There is no way to tell. She could sleep until tomorrow, or she might slumber for a year and a day."

"It little matters, either way," he sighed. "My father has been recalled. I must accompany him home."

"Does your father know?" Lady Ennallya asked.

There was a long pause. "I haven't told him about the Fellowship nomination."

"That was not the question I was asking, but your answer tells me everything I need to know."

"You talk in riddles, Lady—"

"Lady Ennallya. Tell your father that you've met me. You should not need to tell him anything else."

"Lady Ennallya!" Oramis gasped. "But— You're—"

"As old as the legend, and still working for the Fellowship," she laughed. "Now, it is time for you to leave. What token will you offer so that she knows you plan to return?"

"I didn't expect to be permitted—"

"That fine brooch you have pinned to your chest will serve the purpose," Ennallya said.

"Do you know what this represents?" Oramis asked.

"Of course."

"And yet, you ask?"

"Whether you leave it or not is entirely your decision."

A few moments later, something hard pressed into the sleeper's palm. Oramis folded her fingers over the dragon brooch and kissed her hand. "Farewell, dear Lady," he whispered and then he was gone.

Hoovar vraa waeshaen vraagish.

Phoena floated on the tide...

"Lord Oramis has come and gone," Ennallya announced.

"That was easily done," Cecily replied. "I didn't want him to think that my resistance was diminished because of his fervour."

"I gave him the message for his father," Lady Ennallya said.

"Then we will see what comes of that. I distrust the rumours that are circulating. There's trouble in the outer realms. I fear that circumstances are moving too fast."

Shan oshaan raeshtinn aroear, hoeiabva leststoer rayem.

Phoena dreamt that someone pounded on the door.

"Please let him in," she murmured before drifting deeper beneath the dream river.

"What is the meaning of this disruption?" Lord Westernbrooke shouted.

"I have to see her!" Karilion cried.

"You should have waited for an invitation."

"I know Oramis got to see her before he left, so it's only fair that I receive the same favour."

"Fairness has nothing to do with anything. What is it to me if you're summoned early to the King's Council?"

"Ha! So you know," Karilion muttered. "It's supposed to be a secret. You've confirmed that you have influence at the court. I'm tempted to refuse to go."

"You cannot refuse a summons from your king."

"I would if I were convinced it was only a ruse to get rid of me."

"Hmmph. I'm sure I could find an easier and more permanent way of getting *rid* of *you*," her godfather remarked.

"Well, I'm here now, so you have to let me speak to her."

"You can speak all you like, but don't expect her to

answer you."

Speak Karilion did, and eloquently, but her mind could not hang onto his words. Finally, he seized her hand and slipped an icy object onto her wrist. "I dare not give you magical treasures, dear Lady, so I am leaving you something of more sentimental value. This bangle looks plain, but when it is under the light of the moon, it transforms into a thing of great beauty. Tradition has it that this trinket was formed from a fallen star at the beginning of time."

Vathshar hoei ara kaeng oevar flaeth, ae staell shaell khoei deiy.

Dark replaced the light, an endless cycle without pause. It was dark again...

"The third one is here." This time it was the footman who made the announcement.

"Show Viscount Baraapa in," Cecily said. "You might as well stay, Westy. We could benefit from your assistance should he decide to carry her away."

"He wouldn't dare!" Lord Westernbrooke shouted. Furniture scraped across the polished boards as her godfather leapt to his feet.

"He's heard your warning," Ennallya laughed, "so sit down and behave yourself. Young man, what is your petition?"

"Lord Westernbrooke, Matron, My Lady," Baraapa began. "Please excuse my intrusion. I require your advice."

"So you're not here to steal away my goddaughter?"

"Certainly not," Baraapa cried. "Karilion and Oramis would be after me in an instant. There's nowhere in the world that I could hide her."

"I wouldn't be so certain of that," Ennallya said softly, but nobody seemed to hear her.

"What is your problem?" Cecily asked him.

"My father is coming," Baraapa said.

"That's not unexpected," Cecily replied.

"He has plans to put my new talents to better use. I'm offered a commission in the militia. If my father has his way, I'll be the captain of an elite force, and sent to fight in the colonies by the end of the month."

"You don't wish to fight?" Lord Westernbrooke asked.

"It's not the fighting that I have a problem with. It's whether my leaving will be viewed by the Fellowship as a betrayal. I'm only recently nominated, and now my allegiance is being called away."

"The Fellowship will not see this as a betrayal," Cecily assured him.

"But will Her Ladyship?" the young nobleman cried.

"Ah," Ennallya said. "Here is the truth of the matter. What does your heart tell you?"

"Pardon, My Lady, but we haven't been introduced."

"Lady Ennallya from the Thristian Mountains, at your service, Viscount Baraapa. I've known your family since before your ancestor received his title."

"Have you been with the Fellowship that long, Lady Ennallya?"

"I was there in the beginning. I did not expect that I would still be here, but I am pleased with your nomination. It does my heart good to see that there is still honour among my people."

"Thank you, My Lady."

"Do you have anything to say to our sleeper?" Ennallya asked.

"There is nothing to say that cannot wait until she is awake to hear it."

"At last, a youth with some common sense," muttered Lord Westernbrooke. "I can see that you've made up your mind to accept the military commission, so take your leave."

"Not so fast in dismissing the poor boy," Cecily said. "He still has to present her with his gift."

"Lord Oramis left her his dragon brooch," Ennallya added. "And Lord Karilion gave her a bangle made from a fallen star. What does Viscount Baraapa offer as a token of his allegiance?"

"It is nothing of such value as the other noblemen's gifts," Baraapa said. "Just something that I made with my hands from the fishing tackle the three of us were using that day."

"You included the others in your gift?" Cecily asked. "How interesting. It looks like a fine neck chain with a medallion attached."

"He's made something to help her find her way home," Ennallya replied.

Faenn shooth vath vrail aen thraest thraimon.

It was warm here in the dream. The rhythm between wakefulness and sleeping had changed.

"I don't think it will be long before she awakens," Cecily said. "Her movements have become more restless in the past hour."

"I have already begun packing," Ennallya replied. "Have you given any thought to her wardrobe? She cannot leave here in that nightdress."

"I've dispatched Westy to the capital with an order. I expect him to return with the bare necessities before dinner," Cecily said. "The rest of her new clothes will be waiting for us when we arrive at Sumnarscote."

"The decision is made?" Ennallya asked.

"Indeed. Westy is convinced that having her reside within a day's journey of the King's Citadel is best. He intends to introduce her to general society within the capital. He hopes that it will be a year or two before he must deliver her to the king as the new champion. Westy has recruited other members of the Fellowship to begin her training. In the meantime, arrangements are in place for her to attend the nearby ladies college as a day student. If she is well enough, she starts with the new semester."

"That only gives us four weeks to get her ready."

Khoe shae paell aen shoalaethnass vroet..."

Phoena dreamt that she stood at the top of a mighty waterfall. The spray rose high into the air and soaked her to the skin.

"Phoena." The unknown voice resonated both inside her head and outside in the cool air. It was the voice of her childhood dreams.

"Who calls me?"

"Over time, my name has been translated into many tongues: Vathshar; Kaeng; Deiy. I Am Who I Am. I have called you and watched over you. You have petitioned me for help, and I have answered you."

"Thank you."

"Phoena, it is time for you to return to your commission. Are you ready?"

"Will you continue to guard and guide me?"

The roar of the water was the only reply. Suddenly, Phoena was falling.

She landed heavily and awoke on the floor beside the canopied bed in the guest bedchamber. "That's one way to wake up. But I would have preferred a softer landing."

Lady Ennallya was beside her in a moment, helping her to her feet. "How are you feeling now, Shurma?"

"I'm fully recovered."

"Your godfather left instructions for you to join him in his apartment for dinner, should you wake in time. I'll help you get dressed."

"Your kindness is appreciated, Lady Ennallya."

Phoena stretching her arms above her head. The bangle on her wrist dropped down, and she looked at it with a fond smile. Her hand flew to her throat, where the medallion nestled against her skin. She looked down at her chest in search of the third token.

"The brooch is under your pillow," Ennallya said. "Cecily

was worried that the pin might come undone and pierce your heart."

Lady Ennallya went to the bed and retrieved it. She handed the jewel to Phoena. "Why am I not surprised that your first thoughts are towards your three champions? Although how you could know about their gifts while you were sound asleep, I'm sure I don't know."

Phoena smiled, wrapped her arms around herself, and began to sing: "Shaezz vraa..."

Immediately the whole room seemed brighter. Any doubts and concerns that Phoena had for her uncertain future fled.

Lady Ennallya closed the distance between them to embrace her. "Shurma, you are full of surprises today. One day soon, you will have to tell me your story. I can see that you are destined to steal many hearts, beyond the three you already have in your possession. It pleases this old woman to add my allegiance to theirs. Lady Firebird, welcome to the Fellowship."

THE END
OF BOOK 1

CHARACTER LIST

Phoena (16) aka Fee aka Lady Firebird
>   servant girl at *Westernbrooke Academy for Young Noblemen*

Lord Oramis (21) – international student and nobleman
>   His father is an ambassador

Viscount Baraapa of Larimore (17)
>   international student and nobleman

Virago & Virtuo of Grandeheill (17)
>   Baraapa's friends, international students, junior nobility

Lord Karilion of Hemington (17)
>   local nobleman, heir to position on the King's Council

Matron aka Cecily (45) – In charge of household staff
>   responsible for student wellbeing

Headmaster Pepperbry
>   current headmaster at *Westernbrooke Academy*

Heilga (29) – senior maid, Fee's only friend

Lord Westernbrooke aka Westy – Phoena's godfather
>   founder and previous headmaster of *Westernbrooke Academy*

Draggo Oramis
>   father to Oramis, Emberite Ambassador

Hampton – *Westernbrooke Academy* stableman

Lady Ennallya
>   member of the Fellowship, from the Thristian Mountains

Shurma – term of endearment
Sumnarscote & Thristian Mountains – two locations mentioned

FANTASY RIVER SERIES

PHOENA'S QUEST 2: SECOND FLAME
(COMING IN 2021)

The quest is almost complete, yet the mysterious flame remains hidden. And darkness reigns...

Phoena's servant life is over. No more scrubbing floors and picking up after spoilt young noblemen. Goodbye to being the target for their experimental magic. She is determined to enjoy her freedom, but will fourteen years' service be the right preparation for the all-girls College she is to attend?

That should be the least of her concerns: there is another champion be found. Phoena hopes the selection process will be uncomplicated. But a chance encounter with Lady Nessandra, the most eccentric student at the College, threatens everything. Nessie's rash decisions activate Phoena's magical talent in new ways, and the outcome is unpredictable.

Can Phoena keep her identity a secret? What will become of this quest if her awakening magic overwhelms her? Read on to find out if Phoena is ready for the coming adventure.

PHOENA'S QUEST 3: THIRD FIRE (LATE 2021)

Five champions have been selected to accompany Phoena on her quest. An ancient prophecy, a political storm, and an unexpected threat from across the seas draw Phoena and her friends into a contest that will cost one of them everything

OTHER BOOKS

At first glance, Phoena's story has little in common with my other boo. Phoena's world is one where magic and fantasy are an accepted part of everyday life, and the *River Wild* stories are set in contemporary Australia.

But Phoena's world began as a dream sequence in the first *River Wild Romantic Suspense Novel: White Rose of Promise*. I have included an excerpt from that story here:

page 57 (*White Rose of Promise,* paperback edition, 2019)

Ria was certain she was dreaming. All around her, swirling rainbows of light flashed in harmony with waves of pain. This breaking surf was drawing her down into a blue whirlpool. She tried to open her eyes, and the world exploded in a galaxy of iridescent stars. A strange darkness enveloped her like a raging torrent, then the pain faded to a distant memory.

Nothing remained but the heavy darkness. Now she floated, a soothing river bearing her gently towards a distant light. The glimmer turned into a glow. This grew until it burned like holy fire and consumed everything else. Her heart responded to the light, and she knew she was in the presence of God. Now on her feet, she was surrounded by crystal purity, overcome by a peace beyond description.

The fantasy river makes an appearance in each of the stories, which also include dreams and visions, prophesy and wondrous signs. Each of the books in the *River Wild Romantic Suspense series* feature the river as an important element that leads to character transformation.

River Wild
Romantic Suspense Series

These books can be read in any order. Each story stands alone, but some of the characters make an appearance in every story.

Available at www.chrissygarwood.com

Book 1 (2019) *White Rose of Promise*
Book 2 (2019) *When Promises Are Broken*
Book 3 (2020) *When Freedom is Promised*
Book 4 (2020) *Which Promise This Time?*
Book 5 (2021) *When Promises Are Forever*
Book 6 (2021) *Waiting For A Promise*
Book 7 (2021-22) *Who Pays The Piper?*

White Rose of Promise

A prophetic dream she can't remember. A shameful past she can't forget. An impossible future she dare not cherish.

Maria Evangelina Fontana* comes home from twenty years in exile. She is looking for reconciliation but her family refuse to acknowledge the secret that keeps them apart. They cannot accept that the lost years have changed her forever. Her hope for a new beginning fades.

Sebastian Romano has no time for women and abhors weakness. The wealthy businessman is uncertain why he offers Ria* a way out of her dilemma, but it is too late to change his mind. If only he had understood the risk.

Ria's innocence turns his orderly world upside down. Her faith challenges his values as she steps into her destiny. He thought he was done with his violent past, but his enemies have found her. Romano watches helplessly as the prophecy unfolds...

When Promises Are Broken

A family curse, an evil plot, an unlucky coincidence. Three destinies entwined.

Sofia sits in angry isolation at the wedding reception, unspoken secrets and broken promises her only consolation. No-one will listen, and now it is too late. Her innocent sister has married a very bad man.

Pastor John Edwards is puzzled by Sofia's animosity. Her emotional outburst drives him to prayer. When a sinister stranger warns him to keep his distance, he wonders if it is already too late.

Valentino makes clear what he wants from Sofia. He is rich, handsome and available. So why does she question his motives and reject his advances? He laughs at her assertion that trouble pursues her, but then he disappears...

When Freedom Is Promised

An unlucky coincidence? A fiendish plot? Or a sacred design that promises freedom?

Bad things happen to good people. Abigail is on the run, anxiety and fear her constant companions. She must survive to testify and needs a place to hide. Her new identity comes with the assurance that her enemies will not seek her in Melbourne. Could it be the answer to her prayers?

Freddie's nephew has disrupted his orderly life. After a decade cut off from his family, his loneliness awakens. But the angry teenager's violence is only the beginning.

When the boy and Abigail collide, her cover is blown. Her relentless enemies are coming. But Freddie is in their way. Can Abigail forget past betrayals and learn to trust this gentle stranger? Will Freddie risk everything to set her free?

When Promises Are Forever

Sara Messinger has a crush on her boss, Nero Mariani. When she meets Oliver Johnston, a *Maximum Security* agent, he warns her to be careful. Oliver knows that Nero's family business is not what it seems. Has Oliver's warning come too late? Nero's influential family want to find him a replacement wife, and Sara seems like the perfect candidate.

ACKNOWLEDGEMENTS

This book could not have been written without the support and encouragement of many people.

Firstly, I am grateful to God for inspiring me, for giving me the time and the persistence to bring this story into life.

My writing adventure has not been a solitary one. God provided me with a supportive team - determined to ask the right questions to keep me moving forward. Thanks to Naomi McGlone, Katisha & Trish O'May, Ray Woodrow, Danielle Campbell, Eva Bitterova, Belinda McGuire, Tim Berry, and Donna Bullen for your help with *PHOENA'S QUEST 1: FIRST SPARK*

I am thankful for you, dear reader. I hope you have enjoyed meeting Phoena and her friends, and that you will return to find out what happens in the next instalment.

A special thanks to Belinda Pollard, publishing mentor and editor, for taking me under her wing and for the professional advice that has helped make this book better than I could have imagined.

Last but not least, thanks to my patient husband Tony, for his constant encouragement, and ongoing support.

Chrissy